A Soldier's Heart

SHERRILL BODINE

Diversion Books
www.DiversionBooks.com

DIVERSIONBOOKS

*To the super-support group for the friendship, advice,
prodding, and courage.*

Diversion Books
A Division of Diversion Publishing Corp.
443 Park Avenue South, Suite 1008
New York, New York 10016
www.DiversionBooks.com

Copyright © 1991 by Elaine Sima and Sherrill Bodine
All rights reserved, including the right to reproduce this book or portions
thereof in any form whatsoever.

This is a work of fiction. Names, characters, places and incidents either are the
product of the author's imagination or are used fictitiously. Any resemblance
to actual persons, living or dead, events or locales is entirely coincidental.

For more information, email info@diversionbooks.com

First Diversion Books edition December 2013.
Print ISBN: 978-1-62681-609-1
eBook ISBN: 978-1-62681-207-9

Book One

Book One

The Meeting

LONDON SEASON, 1813

Lord Matthew Blackwood stood in the wide, rectangular doorway leading into Lady Charlesworth's ballroom and took one cursory glance at the *ton* at play. Only Kendall's insistence they obey Her Grace's dictate to stop by before going on to White's had induced him to waste even a few hours of leave enduring the grueling tedium of such a sad crush. On the passage from the Peninsula, Kendall had prosed on and on about the activities they must throw themselves into while at home—boxing at Gentleman Jackson's, races at Newmarket, cockfights in the country. Dancing attendance at *ton* balls was not Matt's idea of a desirous diversion to take his mind from the battlefield. The petticoat line was Kendall's, perhaps even his brother Longford's, world, certainly not his. He knew exactly what he was looking for; the trouble was, he was beginning to think she didn't exist.

Bored already, he half turned toward Kendall and his gaze fell on a vision. Her ebony hair fell from a topknot in loose ringlets about her perfect oval face. Her wide, blue eyes dominated her tiny nose and sweet cherry lips. Her demure white crepe gown fell gently over just-hinted-at delectable curves. She was the embodiment of soft, innocent sweetness he'd dreamed of for years.

"My God, Kendall! She's here!" Matt breathed, unable to contain his excitement, to quite believe she actually existed as flesh and blood. "I've been seeking her and here she is!"

"What are you raving about, Matt?" Lord William Kendall, dressed in the identical rifle green of their brigade, had also been idly glancing about the room, but now straightened to attention.

"There!" Impatiently he directed Kendall's wandering eye. "The raven-haired angel next to Lady Charlesworth. She must be her niece, Miss Serena Fitzwater."

"Yes, a pretty little thing." Kendall shrugged. "But this season, fair hair is the rage, I'm told. We've six weeks of leave, at best, before it's back to old Picton's tyranny, so might as well dally with nothing but diamonds of the first water."

"Old friend, you don't understand." Clasping Kendall's shoulder, Matt flashed him a brilliant smile. "Before I return to the Peninsula, I plan to make that angel my bride."

"Matt, are you mad!"

His friend's astonished face proved no deterrent. Matt always knew exactly what he wanted, and once his mind was made up, he allowed nothing to distract him. The powers of concentration that made him an excellent soldier would stand him in good stead for the coming battle of hearts.

Making his way across the packed ballroom floor, he barely noticed the interested looks that marked his direction. Nor did he pay much heed to the whispered admiration that followed him. He blocked out the dozens of flickering candles in tall silver sticks, the crystal chandeliers blazing overhead, the strains of the waltz played by musicians hidden in the balcony, and the scent of flowers perfuming the air.

All was as nothing beside the perfect vision of Miss Serena Fitzwater. Even her name conjured up delights he'd only dreamed about.

Boldly he stepped before her. Her dark, feathery eyelashes fluttered upward, and at once he was caught in the pure blueness of her sweet gaze. Before, his mind had been captured by seeing his vision brought to life; now his heart gave one single stroke to forge his fate.

Sensing someone pause before her, Serena looked up instinctively to find herself gazing into a young, handsome face—the face of her dreams.

Her fingers trembled so, she clasped them more securely around the silver stem of the nosegay Aunt Lavinia had presented her with, to bolster her courage, and perforce to give her something to occupy her hands this evening. He smiled and the trembling bolted to her middle, making it a trifle difficult to breathe. His smile transformed the handsome face into a startling male beauty never before seen in Serena's small world.

The candlelight haloed patterns of gold in his rich, chocolate hair, and his eyes, an even deeper brown, gazed at her with such intensity; she felt rather light-headed. For the first time in her life, she could relate to the fainting heroines she'd read about, who swooned at the slightest provocation.

This would definitely not do for Reverend Bartholomew Fitzwater's daughter from Market Weighton, East Riding, York! Parsons' offspring were supposed to be made of sterner stuff!

It was with breathless gratitude that Serena heard her aunt's booming voice through the blood pounding in her ears.

"Lord Blackwood, isn't it? What a pleasure to have you home from the wars, and to find you here at our little gathering." Aunt Lavinia gushed as only she could, her chubby face wreathed in a smile.

"Good evening, Lady Charlesworth." His deep voice vibrated with strength as Serena had known instinctively it would. Then he bowed, lifting her aunt's beringed fingers ever so briefly to his firm lips. She was fascinated by his slightest movement, overwhelmed by his courtly courtesy and distinguished air. A hero of the Peninsula, here at her ball. It was almost too much.

"…Mother sends her warmest regards and regrets she could not be in attendance," he was saying.

"Dear Regina! I shall send her a missive the instant she and the duke arrive in town. It is still shockingly light for the opening of the Season, but so many of our more eligible parties are away in those dreadful Peninsular Wars. So fortunate you are home, and I believe I saw another soldier come in with you. I was just saying to—"

Knowing Aunt Lavinia's habit of rattling on at length, often leaving her listener slightly glassyeyed, Serena did the only thing a well-brought-up young woman could do. Very carefully easing her foot from beneath the deep ruffle of her white gown, she slid it under her aunt's puce satin hem until she could very gently trod on Lavinia's slippered toes.

Aunt Lavinia's slightly bulgy eyes widened, her darkened lashes nearly touching her brows. "Ahhh … as I was saying, so happy you are here so I may introduce you to my niece, Miss Serena Fitzwater," she continued with a smoothness that inspired admiration.

Serena received the full power of a smile made dazzling by deepening the dimple in his square chin and darkening his eyes to near ebony.

"Serena, dear, it is my pleasure to make known to you Lord Matthew Blackwood, son of my dear friends, the Duke and Duchess of Avalon. Lord Blackwood is on leave from the Peninsula, where he has distinguished himself."

Lord Matthew Blackwood; at last a name to put to this man who seemed to have stepped right from her dreams. Instead of her usual shy curtsy, Serena extended her hand. She wasn't surprised at Aunt Lavinia's short, not quite suppressed, gasp of shock. She was never so bold. Whatever had come over her?

Her boldness was rewarded. Lord Blackwood raised her hand to his lips and she felt a delicious tingle all the way up her arm when he pressed a correct kiss upon her fingertips.

"Miss Fitzwater, may I have the pleasure of the next waltz?"

As if he had commanded it—and Serena never doubted he could do so, for he appeared so magnificent and all-powerful in his green uniform, whose epaulets emphasized his already broad shoulders—the soft strains of a waltz floated through the air.

For just an instant fear froze her to the spot. Never had she been held in any man's arms but dear Papa's, and that only when they had practiced dance steps in the small parlor of the rectory. But she had been well schooled by Lavinia and forced herself to put her timid hand on his proffered arm, allowing him to lead her into the waltz.

She was rigid with nerves for the entire first circle of the floor. But he seemed so confident, his arms so strong and his steps so sure, that after a few minutes her nervous flutters were calmed. Tentative steps became a familiar pattern, and when she ceased to concentrate, she found she was actually enjoying the whirl around the ballroom. She looked up into his face, expecting him to be glancing beyond her left ear, as Papa always had. Instead he was watching her intently. The oddest sensations assailed her. Sensations Reverend Fitzwater's daughter should rightfully know nothing about; but since the squire's niece had kept her supplied with quite shocking novels purchased on her last trip to London, Serena had discovered a vast streak of romance in her usually sedate nature.

Papa would be shocked to know that sometimes she spun daydreams during his more lengthy sermons. In her romantic fancies her hero would have fair curls or raven black locks, like the novels she'd read. Lord Blackwood's rich brown waves put those to shame. And, sometimes, the eyes gazing down at her with such speaking emotion were blue like her own, or a delicate spring green. Lord Blackwood's deep chocolate eyes eradicated all memory of her visions.

"Where have you been all my life, Miss Serena Fitzwater?" he whispered, causing that deep cleft to mark his chin. "I've been waiting for you, you know."

If she could pinch herself, she would. Was she dreaming? Was she lying tucked in bed upstairs in the rectory, reading by candlelight, her Bible handy in case Papa peeked in and caught her? These were the romantic words of a hero from those deliciously daring novels. Unfortunately she couldn't recall what she should reply. So she simply spoke the truth.

"I've been at the rectory in Market Weighton, Lord Blackwood."

"Well, you are here now, my angel. And I swear I shall never let you go away from me now I've found you."

There was that air of command in his words which made her quite certain he would do exactly as he promised. That notion sent a shiver down her spine. Fortunately the waltz ended and she could step out of his arms before he felt her trembling.

He left her at her aunt's side with a bow that promised his swift return. Her heart pounded in her throat, and although she knew it wasn't proper, her eyes followed him across the ballroom where he fell into animated conversation with another gentleman in identical regimentals.

With a quelling look from beneath her delicately painted brows, and a soft "Harumph," Aunt Lavinia brought Serena back to her senses. She had no time for more wild, romantic notions as her aunt, with booming gusto, presented the next guest.

Very properly, Serena relegated Lord Blackwood to the back of her mind as she went about the business of the ball. For weeks Aunt Lavinia had taught her the proper use of fan and eyelashes, the essentials lacking in a motherless upbringing. Serena had thought them all a trifle silly until she realized with a judicious flick of her fan she could locate Lord Blackwood among the dancers and watch him for a few moments without being detected.

During a country dance with Mr. Herring, Serena could think of nothing but Lord Blackwood's wonderful eyes gazing at her with such warmth. And the set with Baron Shurwood was entirely taken up with her conjectures about Blackwood's strange words … He wouldn't let her go away from him … Whatever could he have meant?

She hadn't long to wait before he presented himself for a second dance. This time she was much more at ease, going through the forms with lighter steps than usual, buoyed by a quite unfamiliar excitement.

"Miss Fitzwater of Market Weighton, what think you of London?" he whispered when they came together shoulder to shoulder in a form, making the dance floor seem as if it held only the two of them.

"It is quite different than home, Lord Blackwood."

They separated, but a moment later, now face-to-face, he leaned toward her, studying her quite seriously, as if her answer was of vital import. "If you miss Market Weighton, what part of it would you wish with you in London to make you content?"

The slight whimsy in his voice and that dimple marking his chin mesmerized her so completely, all her aunt's warnings vanished from her mind. "Besides Papa and Mrs. Buckle, our housekeeper, I miss our garden. But London is so magnificent, it is hard to be homesick! It is so large and there are so many wonderful sights. I don't know how I shall ever see them all!"

Suddenly realizing she had done the forbidden, displayed unfettered excitement where Aunt Lavinia had dictated languid boredom, Serena bit her lower lip, an unfortunate childhood habit never quite overcome.

"I mean, of course, I am enjoying the Season even though it is all a sad crush, is it not?" she finished, trying to ape her aunt's die-away air.

He flung back his head, his laughter rich and full, causing the forgotten flutters to reappear and settle firmly in her middle.

"Well done, Miss Fitzwater. Utterly charming, just as I knew you would be," he whispered quite daringly into her ear, stirring the curls there, under cover of the crowd moving off the floor.

Back beside her aunt once again, he bowed. "Thank you, Lady Charlesworth, for a perfect evening."

Then, without another word, he spun on his heels and was gone, leaving the ballroom strangely empty.

"Very interesting," Aunt Lavinia commented, her owl eyes slitted in a most untypical speculation. "And very proper. Three dances would have drawn unwanted attention, but two were just the thing. Whoever would have thought you would draw the attention of a duke's son? Even a second son!"

"Aunt Lavinia, what—" Serena wanted to ask what she meant, but was cut off precipitately.

"Sometimes, Serena, you amaze even me!" Aunt Lavinia's huge blue orbs gazed at her fondly. "You're usually so insipidly proper, just as one would expect from your father's daughter, and then, tonight, you do something positively inspired like extending your hand to Blackwood. And trodding on my toes to lead me to the proper point. Your father was never so subtle as that when we were children. But those days are long gone and now he's turned into a saint." She sighed. "It's difficult being a proper sister to your papa, Serena. If only I knew exactly what would please him most."

"Papa only wishes me to be happy, Aunt Lavinia." Serena spoke up quickly, hoping to get a word in. "May I ask why you find Lord Blackwood's conduct so interesting?"

"Because, Serena, he is definitely catched! How interested is the question?" she mused, at once looking like an overstuffed owl, wreathed in a smile.

There was no question in Serena's mind about her own interest. Yet during all her daydreams about this night, which had seemed nothing more than impossible a few months ago in Market Weighton, never could she have imagined it more perfect than Lord Matthew Blackwood had made it.

The Courtship

"Serena, wake up at once!"

The insistent voice interrupted a particularly pleasant dream: Lord Blackwood was sweeping her up in his arms, about to enter a bedchamber. It was probably just as well the dream ended abruptly, because the novels were somewhat vague about what happened next.

"Serena, child!" The booming voice came again.

Slowly Serena forced her reluctant lids open. The sight of Aunt Lavinia, her graying hair falling about her shoulders, clad in nothing but a ruffled jonquil dressing gown, brought her bolt upright in bed.

"Aunt Lavinia, what is amiss? Papa?" she gasped, her sleep-numbed mind grasping at what might be the only logical reason for her aunt to be out of bed at such an unseemly hour.

"No! This!" She flung open the bedchamber door to admit three upstairs maids and two downstairs maids, each carrying an enormous bouquet. Yellow primroses, pink gillyflowers, blue cornflowers, white and red roses, filled their arms. Two giggled self-consciously.

"Don't gabble about there. Back to your duties." Lavinia waved her hand in dismissal before rounding on Serena. "There is even more downstairs. A veritable garden! The house is abuzz, so my maid woke me, knowing full well I would want to immediately discover who is so extravagantly courting you." She thrust a cream envelope under Serena's nose. "Here! Open it at once."

Serena did as she was bid, even though she already guessed who had sent them. It was confirmed a moment later as she gazed down at bold black handwriting.

"A piece of your garden to ease thoughts of home. Until we meet again. Blackwood." Serena folded the note over in her palm and looked up into her aunt's startled face.

The owl-like eyes stretched so wide in surprise, Serena feared it must be painful. When Aunt Lavinia demanded a chair, Serena scrambled out of bed to assist her.

She collapsed into the fragile gilt chair, muttering to herself. "What could the boy be about?"

Standing barefoot in her night shift, Serena hovered over her, the precious note clasped securely in her fist. "Aunt Lavinia, are you all right?"

Lavinia seemed to collect herself. "All right! My dear girl, a duke's son! And not just any, but Avalon. And a chance to be a duchess; for the heir, the Marquess of Longford, is such a dissolute hellion, he's bound to come to an untimely end. Then...! Oh, I can hardly stand the sheer pleasure of informing your dear papa how brilliantly I have launched you."

Surging to her feet with an energy Serena had never before witnessed, Aunt Lavinia clasped her in a snug, lavender-scented embrace. "After breakfast we will return to Madame Bretin's for at least two more evening dresses."

"But I thought we had spent all the money Papa had allotted?"

"Penny-pinching was fine when I thought you could look no higher than a baron. But now we must spare no expense! Be ready in two hours," she commanded, before sailing out of the room triumphantly.

Alone, the delicate mingled scents of bouquets the maids had placed on all the surfaces surrounding her, Serena clasped her hands together. Could Aunt Lavinia be right? Had Blackwood been as shaken by their meeting as she? He was a soldier, a distinguished one according to her aunt. Could he be laying siege to her heart? She chewed unconsciously on her bottom lip as she bent over the cornflowers. Had he known they were nearly the same color as her eyes?

She had no time to spin romantic dreams! Really, she must get a grip on her absurd new fancies! She knew why she was in London for a Season: it was her duty to make a good match which would enhance her family lines. She was the granddaughter of a baron, niece to the present Baron Fitzwater, a niece by marriage to the late Lord Charlesworth, and cousin to the present, Frederick. Although her lineage was not as old and noble as some, she had her place in the *ton* and her duty to perform.

That that duty would make her heart pound in her throat and turn her icy cold yet too warm at the same time had never entered her head. At least, not until she'd put aside the weighty books on sermons and religious philosophy which had made up most of her reading matter and daringly took up her first novel. In truth, the fragile idea of a love match had only flitted through her mind then. Now, she admitted, since being bowled over by Lord Blackwood, the idea had taken wing.

Despite her better intentions, she was still sitting, musing, when a gentle knock upon the door heralded the maid's entrance with her usual breakfast of hot chocolate and dry toast. Spurred into action, she sipped and nibbled as she hastily performed her toilette so as to not keep Aunt Lavinia waiting.

They arrived in the entrance hall at the precise moment, and Serena stood quietly while Aunt Lavinia gave her appearance a thorough appraisal. Serena had taken great pains to get the white plume on her flat gray hat to curl just so. She was rewarded with a smile.

"You will do quite nicely, Serena," her aunt declared. "But I believe one more walking costume is also in order."

Aunt Lavinia was a woman of her word, Serena discovered. Whereas before, the rose silk had been too dear to consider making into an evening dress, now it had to be completed immediately, plus a scarf with spangles added as a drape about Serena's shoulders. Another gown of a blue nearly identical to her eyes was declared a must by Madame Bretin and agreed to. A walking costume in the shade *minuit* and a perky hat with wide satin ribbons was added. There seemed to be no limit to Aunt Lavinia's extravagance.

Apparently satisfied, her aunt rose from the chair Madame

Bretin had provided, but sat rather firmly down when the modiste draped silk shot through with silvery threads over Serena's shoulders.

Aunt Lavinia blinked several times. "It does do wonders for her pale skin. And against those ebony curls…" The owl eyes slitted as she pondered for long moments, unconcerned that Serena was standing in nothing but her shift.

Madame Bretin considered three or four plates before selecting, a shrewd look in her eye. "This style for Mademoiselle, I believe, to show off her fine shoulders and bosom."

Finally Aunt Lavinia nodded. "It shall be the pièce de résistance. The very thing for Lady Sefton's ball. It must be finished by this Friday."

"But of course," Madame Bretin promised, clapping her hands.

Two shopgirls hurriedly carried away bolts of fabric while another helped Serena back into her gray dress, which, in comparison, seemed lifeless and dowdy. She ran her hands over the proper costume Papa had made up for her trip to London. It had seemed the finest gown she'd ever owned.

Turning away from her reflection, she tried to regain her perspective. What would Papa think? Her dress was made of good fabric and would wear well, much more practical than the fine silks she'd just chosen. She hadn't even read the daily passages from her Bible since arriving in London. She had, instead, concentrated on following Aunt Lavinia's dictates for a successful Season: how to curtsy gracefully; how to hide behind her fan when flirting; and, most important—perfecting a bored expression amidst the balls and soirees, never allowing anything so vulgar as emotion to show. This, Serena couldn't quite master. Now, suddenly, she wished for dear Papa and his wise counsel, and Buckle's gentle understanding.

"Hurry now, Serena, I want you to rest this afternoon so you'll be in prime looks tonight," Aunt Lavinia urged, hastening back to their waiting coach. "The pink satin, I think, very springish and…"

The bustle of activity on Bond Street caused Serena to stop

and look around her. Members of the *ton* promenaded both sides of the street: ladies in beautiful walking ensembles, bucks in shining Hessians, and dandies, their shirt points so high, they could turn their heads neither right nor left. The street itself was clogged with crested carriages, and a high-perched phaeton clipped past, pulled by a matching pair of blacks, a small tiger clutching the rear fender. There was an excitement in the very air which called to something inside her, something that must have been only waiting, dormant, during all the peaceful years growing up alone in the rectory at Market Weighton.

"Do stop daydreaming, Serena, and get into the coach!" Aunt Lavinia whispered sharply.

Serena realized she was blocking the sidewalk and dutifully climbed up beside her aunt.

"Really, Serena, do be more attentive! Tonight might be a turning point in Blackwood's regard. I must gauge him carefully." Her aunt's face was uncharacteristically stern, her huge eyes almost hard. "I promise you I won't let this opportunity slip away from you. I would be utterly lacking in familial feeling if I did anything but my utmost to bring Blackwood up to scratch!"

With rare insight Serena knew nothing her aunt or she could do would alter what was to come. Lord Blackwood had said he would not let her go. Serena believed him.

Matt's first maneuver of sending Serena every posy he could find at such short notice had its desired result. When she entered Lady Farnsley's ball, her gaze immediately searched him out even in the midst of one of the saddest crushes he'd ever seen. He fought his way across the crowded room, barely acknowledging greetings now that his objective was in sight.

Tonight she was again the picture of his dream, her ebony curls gathered in bunches over each shell-like ear, framing the sweet innocence of her face. A soft pink color flushed her cheeks as he presented himself.

"Miss Fitzwater, you look especially lovely tonight." Although she did not offer her hand, he took it nonetheless, raising it to his mouth and letting his lips linger on her long, thin fingers a moment more than he should. She gazed at him with such earnest bewilderment—obviously an innocent—that he squeezed her hand hearteningly once before releasing it.

"You are very kind, Lord Blackwood. Thank you for the lovely flowers. They are quite wonderful," she responded in correct form, receiving an almost imperceptible nod from her aunt.

Lady Charlesworth had always reminded Matt of a giant owl with her gray hair and huge, knowing eyes, which now pinned him with cool calculation. "Lord Blackwood, it is so close in here. Perhaps Serena would enjoy an orangeade on the terrace."

With a jolt of surprise, Matt realized reinforcement was at hand. Obviously Lady Charlesworth supported his campaign. But did she realize how quickly Serena must surrender her heart?

"An excellent idea, Lady Charlesworth. May I escort you to the terrace, Miss Fitzwater?"

At her blushing nod, he placed her hand on his arm and guided her through the throng out onto the terrace.

The music and voices left behind, quiet closed about them. He settled her in a corner, out of a slight breeze which chilled the evening air. Her scarf slid from her shoulders. As he reached to adjust it, inadvertently his fingers brushed across her throat just above the soft rise of her breasts.

Her gasp stilled his hand and he stepped back before the sudden blaze in her eyes.

"Are you attempting to seduce me, Lord Blackwood?"

Shock rooted him to the spot. He knew her background— the only child of Reverend Bartholomew Fitzwater, second son of the third Baron Fitzwater. How could the gently bred, inexperienced girl he knew her to be even think such a thing?

"No, Miss Fitzwater," he finally found voice to utter. "I've been away from London a long time, but I don't believe custom has changed so much that it would be at all the thing to do at Lady Farnsley's ball."

"I am untutored in London ways, but it seems your actions verge on the bold, my lord." She stared up at him with huge blue eyes, her hands clutched in her lap as demurely as if she were sitting in a pew at her father's church. "You are a soldier and must return to your duties soon. Are you hoping for a dalliance? If so, I fear it cannot be."

How adorable she was! Delight replaced shock. His perfect English flower had the gift of honesty, a trait he prized above all others. But if she already thought him bold, he might as well continue. Lifting both her hands, he turned them palm up, pressing kisses into each center. "Miss Fitzwater, before I return to the war, I mean to make you my bride."

"Your bride?" she gasped, pulling her hands free so one could flutter nervously at her throat. "But you don't even know me."

"I know you're the woman I've been hoping to find."

"You have been looking for someone approximately my height, with dark hair and blue eyes?"

Her earnestness caused him to smile. "As a matter of fact, yes, you are exactly what I've been seeking."

"You mean someone with my background: a parson's daughter, reared in the country," she persisted with quiet dignity.

In battle Matt knew only cool certainty, but confronted with Serena's calm logic, he became slightly agitated. "It has nothing to do with your background. I only know the instant I saw you, I wanted you for my bride."

Tilting her head, she chewed on her lower lip for a minute as she studied him. "It seems to me, Lord Blackwood, you are in the clutch of a romantic vision."

"Nay, Miss Fitzwater, you are the woman I truly want to make my own." Pressing his advantage, as she continued to calmly study him with clear eyes, Matt reached for and again lifted her hand, holding the palm up in his fingers. "My boldness will know no bounds to achieve my end. I pray you won't dash my hopes so soon."

Determined to win her heart no matter the odds, he was confident of the outcome, so was shocked to discover his pulse raced waiting for her answer.

"Your hopes are safe with me, Lord Blackwood," she

whispered, dropping her eyes.

Elated at her response, he covered her small hand with his other and drew it once more to his lips. "Just as your heart will be safe with me."

Enthusiasm prevailed over reason and he led Serena out for three waltzes. He knew tongues would wag, but that was of little import. The sooner the whole world realized his happiness, the better.

He pressed his campaign the next evening at the Countess North's soiree. His attentions marked Serena yet were not so scandalous as to draw censure upon her.

When he stayed continuously at her side, two nights later at the Duchess of Monmouth's musicale, and cheerfully discouraged other suitors by escorting her down to supper, the wags were certain.

By the next morning the on-dit of the *ton* was that he had run mad. The betting book at White's carried a wager he would be wed within a fortnight. So it came as no surprise when his brother, the Marquess of Longford, strolled idly in while Jeffries, his batman, was still shaving him.

"Be careful with that razor. Best to keep sharp instruments away from my young brother. He's run mad, you know," Longford drawled, sprawling in a chair, his legs stretched out before him.

"Aye, Master Matt has run mad," Jeffries growled, carefully cleansing the shaved cheeks with a hot towel, successfully muffling Matt's attempt to reply. "Never been in the petticoat line, now fair makin' a fool of himself over a lass." Shaking his head, Jeffries hastily gathered the bowl of sudsy water, and departed with a loud bang of the door.

"I couldn't have said it better myself." His brother pinned him with eyes as dark as his own. "You'd best explain what is really going on in that idealistic head of yours before I come to my own cynical conclusion."

"Long, it's quite simple. I'm in love." Matt smiled, leaping up to pace the oriental carpet of the room. Being fired with excitement similar to what he felt in battle meant he couldn't contain his energy. "I know you will wish me happy."

"I wish you to come to your senses." The lines of dissipation deepened around Long's firm mouth as his lips twisted in a frown. "You can't love the chit! I've been informed you first laid eyes on her less than a fortnight ago. By George, she's a parson's brat! You, above all people, know you should be looking for someone worthy to be the next Duchess of Avalon. Several bets on at White's I'll come to an untimely end either at the hands of a jealous husband or break my neck riding one of my horses before you receive even a scratch in battle."

Long's voice was so full of bored indifference, a shiver ran down Matt's spine.

"You know I hate it when you talk like this." Matt forced a laugh, determined to let nothing mar his happiness. "You have a strong code of honor, uniquely your own. And you're the finest horseman in all of England. I shall go on the books at White's as betting against such a turn of events. I know you as no one else does. You find amusement at shocking our smug little world, that's all."

"I worry about you, Matt, I really do," Long drawled, swinging one booted leg over the arm of the chair. "You see all of us as you wish us to be, not as we really are. No doubt you're doing the same thing with the bra—lady. I shudder to think what will happen when the scales finally fall from your eyes and you see us frail mortals as we truly are."

"I only see what's in your heart, Long," Matt answered quietly, recognizing a thread in his brother's bored tone that told him how worried he truly was. "Our world is full of wondrous possibilities. Because I embrace those possibilities instead of sneering at them should cause you no concern."

"Zounds, Matt! I suppose in the midst of bloody battle you see only the glory!" Long barked with uncharacteristic anger, unfolding from the chair.

"In the midst of battle your brother thinks of nothing but victory." Kendall laughed, striding in unannounced. "Sorry to interrupt, but Jeffries sent me up. Said perhaps Longford and I, together, can talk some sense into you."

"You're his best friend, Kendall. Even you must see how outrageously naive he is behaving."

"Longford, if you can't talk him out of this campaign, no one can." With a rueful grin, Kendall shrugged his wide shoulders. "If Matt says he loves Miss Fitzwater and has put her on a pedestal, then we can do naught to tumble her."

"Stop it, both of you." Matt kept his voice light, although he was irritated that his two closest friends wouldn't understand how important this was to him. "You're talking like I'm some green youth with my head in the clouds, making a fool of myself over my first calf love."

The speaking look Long turned on Kendall sparked anger in Matt's chest. "Cut line, Long! I'm not your bookish younger brother anymore!"

"No, you are a leader of men, with the courage of martyrs and the ideals of saints. God help us all when you finally join the human race!" With his customary lazy stroll, he reached the door. "Keep an eye on our idealist, Kendall. I'm off for a race to Richmond on my new stallion. If the gamesters are correct, I'll more than likely break my fool neck. Perhaps Matt will have time to come to his senses before it's too late."

As the door clicked shut, Kendall ran his fingers through his sandy curls. "Longford sounds a bit reckless today."

"Long is never reckless. He's simply bored. He shall win his race, never fear." Matt shrugged into his coat, flicking a speck of lint from the arm. He didn't want Kendall to know how deeply Long's words had pierced him. He was not a saint, nor a martyr. He simply chose to see the best in those around him. He expected excellence, and his men gave him just that; it was as much as any soldier could ask.

Clasping Kendall's shoulder, he smiled, letting this slight blemish on his contentment fade away. "Come, I don't wish to be late for Lady Sefton's ball. Tonight is the night, Kendall. There are only four weeks left before we return to the Peninsula. Barely enough time for the banns to be read and a honeymoon at Avalon Landing."

The light sprinkle of freckles across Kendall's patrician

nose stood out starkly as he paled. "Matt! Leg-shackled? Are you sure this is what you want?"

"Never more so. Come. My destiny waits!"

To Matt, it seemed she was waiting. For the instant he crossed Lady Sefton's threshold, despite the flower-festooned ballroom, despite the crush of the aristocracy at play, despite the flickering candlelight, he saw her immediately. Their eyes met and locked.

Tonight she was more beautiful than ever; her ebony curls cascaded over one bare shoulder. Her gown was not as demure as she was used to wearing, for its shimmering beauty made each of her movements appear to be touched by stardust.

Leaving Kendall without a thought, Matt made his way to Serena's side. She greeted him with her usual sweet smile.

"Good evening, Miss Fitzwater." He bowed, resisting the urge to press her fingers to his lips. "Your beauty is beyond words tonight."

His flattery brought the telltale rosy flush to her cheeks and an indulgent chuckle from Lady Charlesworth.

"Lord Blackwood, you have arrived in the nick of time. My dear niece is pining to dance this waltz."

The roses in Serena's cheeks darkened to scarlet. Lady Charlesworth was complaisant in her assumptions, but for once, he didn't mind being outguessed.

With a bow, he took Serena into his arms for the waltz. They fit perfectly, as he knew they would. Each time they were together reaffirmed his belief that she was exactly the woman he'd always dreamed about. Long thought him an idealist, and perhaps he was; but since he was fortunate enough to find his ideal in Serena, why should he waste any more time?

A good soldier knew when to bring matters to a head, so after their second dance, he led her out into Lady Sefton's perennial garden. Other couples could be seen walking along the torchlit crushed-rock paths.

"Shall we stroll, Miss Fitzwater?" He offered his arm, and confidently, or so it seemed to him, she placed her hand, allowing him to guide her through the shadows between the pools of light cast down by the high torches. Strains of a waltz floated through the open French doors and were carried by a breeze to where they stood near a reflection pool. The moment he had been waiting for was at hand.

"May I have this dance, Miss Fitzwater?" His voice softened to a mere whisper.

"Here? Now?" she questioned with a timid smile.

"What could be more perfect than you in the moonlight?"

After a slight hesitation, she nodded. For the first time she leaned into him, resting her cheek against his chest, the magic of the moment apparently affecting his proper English flower as much as it did him. Boldly he settled her even closer, going so far as to rest his lips against the top of her soft, fragrant hair.

"Miss Fitzwater, why are you so quiet this evening?"

Tilting her head back, she gazed up at him. "I've been thinking. It can't be long until you return to the Peninsula."

"Four weeks." He spoke quietly, vaguely noticing the music had stopped, but unwilling to release her from his arms.

"I shall miss you when you are gone," she said with her simple honesty.

"And I you. But I shall leave my heart here in your keeping, for I speak to your aunt tomorrow."

Startled, she stepped away from him. "My lord, you move too quickly!"

"I told you nearly from the first night that I wished you for my bride." Remembering her timid response that his hopes were safe with her, he took her hands. They were trembling. "There's so little time left, Serena, we can't waste it."

Matt's confidence began to fray about the edges as she continued to stare up at him, the silence between them lengthening. He'd had his share of ladybirds and even a brief passionate affair with a Spanish contessa when first he arrived on the Peninsula. But Jeffries had spoken true; he'd never dallied with the young girls of the *ton*. He knew what he wanted and had patiently waited to find her. Now that he had, he would cherish Serena always, if she gave him that right.

Emotions chased each other across her pure face, made more starkly beautiful in the moonlight. Finally he read the answer in her eyes.

"I must be mad!" she whispered, her hands clutching his fingers. "Which is no doubt the reason I can find no fault with your request, my lord. Speak to my aunt; your suit will find favor with both her and me."

The strong strokes of his heart pounded against his ribs.

Victory in battle had never been as sweet as hearing her words.

"May I steal a kiss to seal our bargain, Serena?"

In answer, she closed her eyes tightly, tilting her face upwards toward him. Matt could see how stiffly she held her shoulders, as if bracing herself for the unknown.

Ever so gently he cupped them with his hands to reassure her. Leaning over, he brushed her soft, trembling lips, then lifted his mouth for a heartbeat, before pressing a brief kiss on the sweet lips once more. Slowly she opened her eyes, and even in the darkness, Matt was caught in the intense blaze of blue.

No matter what Long said, this was not his nature creating an ideal woman. It didn't matter that they had known one another only a handful of days; Serena called to his heart as none had done before.

"We shall be well mated, Serena; I give you my word of honor," he promised solemnly.

The Union

"Serena, you sly puss!" Lavinia exclaimed, flying into the bedchamber to embrace her with marked enthusiasm. "Does your sainted father know what a remarkable child you truly are? You inspire such admiration, I'm nearly beside myself." She stepped back to study her protégée from toes to curls.

"You have spoken to Lord Blackwood," Serena calmly offered, masking an excitement every bit as marked as her aunt's.

"Talked to him! My dear girl, he waits in the front parlor so he can do the pretty. I stopped on my way upstairs to send a footman posthaste to Market Weighton. Your father must arrive as soon as possible to seal the bargain. A wedding in three weeks! However will I manage it?" Her wide eyes almost filled her face above a satisfied smile.

She had spoken the truth to Blackwood; she had run mad! Parsons' daughters do not throw their bonnets over the windmill in the matter of a few days, thereby forgetting every vestige of common sense they'd ever possessed. She had accused Blackwood of being in the clutches of a romantic vision. But she was no better. Yet in the midst of the wild, romantic thoughts swirling through Serena's mind, there did exist a small center of calmness. Without haste she crossed to the mirror and retied the wide satin ribbon holding back her curls, then smoothed down the skirt of her lemon India muslin. Satisfied that her appearance was all it should be for this momentous occasion, she smiled at her aunt, who still stood in the middle of the room, her hands clasped together and an enraptured expression lighting her face.

"I shall see Lord Blackwood now."

No one had ever fully explained how Serena should behave at this precise moment. Aunt Lavinia and Papa had simply informed her she must do her duty and try to be content in the bargain. Without siblings, and being the oldest of her friends, excepting the squire's niece, who had not, to her knowledge, ever received an offer, she had no example to follow. For an instant she was struck with the same terror she'd felt when she was informed she was to be thrust willy-nilly into a Season, when she'd never even been in London. Of course, she knew of the *ton*, knew she was part of it, but it was so far away, so removed from the simple pattern of her days. London was another world peopled by glorious creatures who had little to do with Serena Fitzwater of Market Weighton. If she'd not been so bold as to take up her first novel, she would never have known what lay ahead of her. No doubt this was the source of the strange serenity at her core; she knew exactly what she should do. The novels told quite boldly what occurred when a young lady accepted an offer of marriage, and recently Serena had formed some ideas of her own.

As if she were the heroine of the story, she held herself stiffly erect and swept into the parlor.

When Lord Blackwood turned from the mantel, she gave him a small smile before seating herself on the green velvet settee. Just as she knew he would, he knelt on one knee before her.

"Your aunt has given me permission to speak. Serena, you know what I ask. Will you be my bride?" He reached boldly for her hand and raised it to his firm lips.

The sense of calmness began to ripple along its edges; his kisses affected her so. His chocolate eyes gazed at her with the same intensity they had when first they met. Now, like then, she felt the tiniest bit giddy, and clung to the calm, settling her world back on its axis. Lord Blackwood was quite simply the most handsome man she'd ever met. In his regimentals he was the very figure of every girl's romantic dream. That he thought her his ideal was such heady stuff, it left her slightly breathless.

However, at her core a little voice nagged—as handsome and dashing as Lord Blackwood was, he was a virtual stranger in all ways that mattered; at least her papa would think so. But her newly discovered romantic streak quickly stifled that voice. Lord

Blackwood called to something hitherto unknown within her, and that, she couldn't ignore.

"Yes, I shall be your bride," she heard herself saying as if reciting words from a book.

The dimple in his square chin deepened and his face was transformed into such stunning male beauty, she felt her world tilt ever so slightly once again. This fabulous hero wanted her. Wouldn't that make all London gasp in surprise?

"Serena, I swear I shall make you happy." He drew her to her feet as he rose from his knee. "I must go to Avalon Hall to inform my parents. By the time I return, your father will have arrived. Will you miss me, sweetheart?" he asked with the whimsical smile that curved his firm mouth in such appealing lines, Serena wished to touch it.

"Yes. Shall we seal our bargain with a kiss?"

Was there a flicker of surprise in his dark eyes? Had she done something amiss? Miss Serena Fitzwater of Market Weighton would never have been so bold, but another side of her was stirring to life. It was a little frightening to realize she'd never even imagined this aspect of her personality, but now its pull was so great, she actually moved one step closer to him.

"I shall truly miss you, Lord Blackwood," she whispered, gazing up at him before, shocked at the strength of her feelings, her lashes fluttered to her cheeks in embarrassment.

His arm shifted about her waist, pulling her gently toward him. Through the thin muslin, her breasts pressed against his chest. His lips brushed hers with the same gentleness as before, and then, for one heartbeat, deepened, sending a swirl of excitement to lodge in her middle. Immediately he stepped back. His eyes were ebony now in a countenance suddenly rigidly stern.

"My dear Serena, our wedding cannot come quickly enough. Farewell, my love." Turning on his heels, her betrothed left her without a backward glance.

Her betrothed.

At last all her composure fled. Before her knees could give way, she sat back down upon the settee. That kiss had been more than a brief touching, pleasant as that was. That kiss had seemed to promise ... what? Serena didn't fully understand it, or her feelings. Chewing on her lower lip, she gazed into space not quite believing what had transpired in a few weeks. Whatever had come over her?

She'd arrived in London a month ago, and instantly the hustle and bustle of the city awakened something dormant inside her. Perhaps it had started even earlier, when she'd sullied the high tone of her mind, as dear Papa would lament. Whatever the cause, she was every day discovering unknown facets of herself. How would Papa deal with Serena's actions? As cowardly as she knew it was, the Reverend Fitzwater's dutiful daughter wished fervently there were some way to avoid finding out.

She had two days of uncomplicated bliss with Aunt Lavinia cosseting her outrageously before she was awakened to the news her father had arrived during the night and was waiting for her in the breakfast room.

With fumbling fingers she rushed through a hasty toilette. She brushed her dark curls, pulling them back at her nape to tie with a blue ribbon, donned his favorite dress of blue and white dimity, which she'd brought from home. Perhaps if she wore all the trappings of the old Serena, he wouldn't notice the changes that she feared he wouldn't understand.

A wave of homesickness washed over her when she saw him sitting at the head of the table consuming his favorite breakfast of kippers and eggs. In that faraway time she'd never have even thought of concealing her feelings from him. Now she was acutely conscious of saying the right words to please him.

Immediately he rose and embraced her in the safe, strong arms that had always been her haven.

"Serena, my dear, I have missed you so." He held her at arm's length, peering over the top of his eyeglasses. "Let me look at you. Yes, your aunt is correct, you are glowing. Even Mrs. Buckle said I must look for this glow of happiness, and certainly it is here. But, my dear, this is all so sudden. Are you sure you are ready for such an important step?"

His myopic blue eyes crinkled at the corners with worry lines. Did he look older—his pale skin so like her own nearly transparent, and his wispy gray hair whiter? Never would she do anything to worry him or cause him pain.

"Papa, I thought you'd be pleased. I've made a good match, according to Aunt Lavinia."

With his usual gentle smile, which Mrs. Buckle confided long ago made some parishioners feel like errant children, he settled her next to him in a chair.

"A brilliant match, my dear. But how can you, on such short acquaintance, know if this is the man with whom you can share your whole life?"

Biting her lower lip, Serena tried to formulate the answer that would please her father. She couldn't possibly tell him Lord Blackwood was quite simply the most handsome and dashing man she'd ever laid eyes on, and although in truth she truly didn't know him, he must be as beautiful inside as out.

"He's a distinguished soldier and is from an excellent family," she offered carefully.

The lines deepened in her father's narrow face as he reached forward to brush back a stray curl from her forehead, much as he'd done throughout her childhood.

"My dear, you have always been such a dutiful child. I hope you did not misunderstand when I talked about your Season. Of course you must marry one day, but this is so soon. I hope your heart is involved."

"I find him very ... pleasing. I'm sure we shall be happy together, Papa." It was quite difficult keeping her voice the calm, steady tone he was accustomed to hearing. Excitement coiled fingers through every part of her body, making her feel the giddy schoolgirl she'd never been. Lord Blackwood was the stuff of romance, which she now knew had little to do with the clearly defined view of life she'd once held.

"My dear, have you discussed where you shall reside? I know Avalon's main seat is in Berkshire. I believe Blackwood's is on the Essex Coast. Will he resign his commission? Are his interests for politics, the land, or is he a scholar?"

Papa's face was so serious, just as it was in the pulpit. She felt the meanest creature alive for feeling this absurd irritation with him. Of course, reality must intrude into the romantic fantasy she'd been floating through since first she looked into Blackwood's wonderful face, but not just yet. As far as she was concerned, the details would surely come later.

"Papa, Lord Blackwood and I haven't discussed such things." She squeezed her father's long fingers. "When he returns to speak with you, all can be settled then."

"Serena, my dear, what have you and Lord Blackwood talked about? I assume in the few brief weeks of this rather, I fear to say, unorthodox courtship you have had long, heartfelt discussions which led to such strong feelings, you are determined to share your lives."

Surely it was just nerves and not Papa's knowing regard that caused her to jump up and go to the sideboard. "Pray excuse me. I'm suddenly famished." Buying time, she opened each silver chafing dish to examine the contents. Truth to tell, she couldn't eat a bite, there were so many flutters in her stomach. Nevertheless she piled her plate with kidneys, poached eggs, and toast laden with marmalade. Returning to her father's side, she gave him a smile, hopeful it would soften the sternness of his thin lips.

"Serena, my dear, are you avoiding my questions? I cannot agree to this union unless I am convinced it is in your best interest."

The idea this new romantic state might disappear as quickly as it had descended brought her up sharply.

"Papa, you sent me here for the sole purpose of making a marriage. That I have accomplished this in a shorter time than you thought possible shouldn't be of import." Realizing the tone of her voice was not felicitous, she stopped, set her plate down, and started again. "Papa, it is my fondest hope you will agree to my becoming Lord Blackwood's bride."

Her chest ached until she realized she was holding her breath as her father studied her over the rim of his glasses. Only when he nodded could she inhale regularly.

"So be it, my dear. You shall have my blessing."

He opened his arms and she went into them gratefully. Now her wonderful romantic dream was safe.

"Can't hardly believe it, laddie. A betrothal party this night, a wedding in a week. Indecent. Aye, it is," Jeffries grumbled, the cloth in his gnarled hands working over Matt's Hessians.

"Jeffries, you're wearing the leather to a nub. Already I can see myself in the things." Matt laughed, too content to let anything unsettle him.

"What's to do when we're off fightin' the Frenchies?" Jeffries barked, with the familiarity of a trusted servant. He rose to his feet, his bowlegs parted, folded his arms across his chest, and thrust his red, stubby beard in the air. "Aye, that's a wee rub, isn't it, laddie? You're a soldier through and through. Heart and soul. When we finish with these Frenchies we'll have those uppity colonists to contend with, mark my words."

Matt spared one glance into the small mirror over the washstand to check his cravat before turning to his batman. "Don't worry, Jeffries, I don't plan to desert my country. I shall always be a soldier; now I shall also have a wife and family. Lots of men are married. We fight not only for honor but to keep our cherished ones safe at home."

"You don't ken. That's the problem wi' young ones..." Jeffries shook his head in despair and glared at him through bushy brows. "Aye, the marquess is a right one. That great noble head of yours is in the clouds!"

"Dare I believe my ears, Jeffries? You haven't agreed with me since I bought that chestnut mare when I was twenty," Longford drawled, making his presence known. He leaned against the bedchamber doorframe, obviously disapproving.

Recognizing the look in Long's hooded eyes, Matt resigned himself to another lecture. "Come to wish me happy, Long? If you wish to ring a peal over me like Jeffries, go away."

"Nonsense. I've come to tell you I've horses at the side

entrance and the yacht waiting at the coast. They say Greece is lovely this time of year. In a word, I'm here to offer escape before it's too late."

"Too late for what?" Kendall asked, striding purposefully through the doorway, a bottle of port in one hand, glasses clutched in the other. "Not too late to have a final drink to Matt's lost freedom before facing the fracas downstairs."

"Kendall, I'm not wed till next week." Matt laughed, taking the bottle to a small table.

"You're well and truly in parson's mousetrap." Kendall shook his head, one sandy curl falling over his bright green eyes. "A betrothal party in your parents' home with the entire *ton* crushed in to wish you happy means no retreat, Matt. Legshackled! Never thought I'd see the day."

When Jeffries handed them each a glass of port, Kendall leaned against the doorframe opposite Longford and raised his glass. "My condolences to Matt. May Longford and I be more fortunate."

"Charming as always, William."

Both Kendall and Long straightened as the Duchess of Avalon appeared.

"Your Grace, my apologies." Kendall bowed deeply, even though a grin still curved his lips.

"No need for false apologies, William. I plan to be there when you must eat your words. Both of you!" she added with a speaking glance at her eldest son, before lovingly cupping his chin with her graceful fingers.

Only when he responded with a careless shrug and a kiss upon her cheek did she float into the room. Her black lace gown set off her white hair, which contrasted dramatically with the bold black eyes her sons had inherited. At fifty-three, the duchess was still a beautiful woman.

"Mother, I fear the party has adjourned to my bedchamber." Matt smiled, kissing her cheek. Instantly he was transported back to childhood by the essence of rose clinging to her. At bedtime, or whenever he was afraid or lonely, he would be comforted within her arms and surrounded by that scent. "I know you haven't come to wear the willow over me."

"Why bother? She knows you for the stubborn idealist you are!" Long barked out, bringing all eyes to where he lounged against the door. "Mother is well versed in the ways of our world. This goes beyond even its usual lunacy."

Recognizing the thread of concern in Long's practiced boredom, Matt stilled his edge of anger, but he wondered when he would cease being the little brother. "Mother, isn't it amazing Long and I had the same tutors, read the same books, attended the same school at Oxford, yet we see our world so differently?"

"My darlings, it is perfectly understandable." Her light, musical laughter healed his anger and even brought a reluctant smile to Long's mocking mouth. "You are both intelligent men who know there is more than one avenue to the same place. Each of your paths is unique, as befits my sons."

"Mother, please! Kendall hasn't realized he is surrounded by bluestockings." Matt couldn't help but smile at his friend's befuddled expression.

"Don't know about paths or avenues, Your Grace," Kendall retorted in all seriousness. "But Matt reads more than any man on the Peninsula. Not just battle plans, but poetry!" He spoke the word as if it were peculiarly loathsome, and Matt couldn't help but feel a slight twinge of embarrassment. "Byron! Can't abide the stuff, myself. Too prosy for my taste."

Her Grace narrowed her eyes, regarding Kendall with that certain expression that boded ill. "I shall send a packet of literature for you to read on your journey back to the Peninsula. The volumes will surely improve the tone of your mind. I expect to discuss them when next we meet, William."

Thoroughly chastened, Kendall could do naught but bow and hastily empty his glass of port the minute she turned back to Matt.

"Have you made any progress in improving the tone of Cecily's mind?" Matt asked, hoping to distract his mother's attention from his hapless friend.

"Speaking of your sister. She's—"

Whatever his mother had been about to say was forever

lost when the subject flew into the room to cast herself upon Matt's chest. He lifted her up in the air, swinging her around, her delightful laughter as musical as their mother's. Six months short of seventeen, Cecily was already a beauty. Next year at her come-out, her thick white gold hair and contrasting sherry eyes would make her a reigning beauty; for now she was still his little sister. Setting her back on her dainty slippers, Matt kissed the tip of her nose before releasing her.

She danced over to Long, who tugged at one long gold curl, which Matt's whirling her about the room had loosened from its rosy ribbon. "When are they letting you put your hair up, brat?"

"Long, it is so vexing! You *must* talk to mother. She says I can't attend Matt's betrothal party because I haven't yet had my come-out."

"Sorry, poppet, Mother's right. It would cause unwanted attention." Matt was shocked his sister would even think of doing anything so unconventional. "Don't be so impatient to grow up. The rules of etiquette may seem silly now, but they're in place for good reason."

Long didn't quite sneer at him, but came close. "And Kendall thinks Byron proses," he drawled. "Listen, brat, meet me on the second-floor landing at ten and I'll bring you a glass of champagne."

"Will you really, Long?" she asked in a breathless little voice. Then she spied Kendall, who had moved to stand next to the armoire as Matt's bedchamber became crowded with family. All playfulness fell from her; a rose to rival her ribbons and the embroidered flowers around the hem of her muslin gown crept up her neck into her cheeks. Nervously twisting her loose curl around two fingers, Cecily curtsied.

"Lord Kendall, I didn't see you. Good evening."

"Good evening to you, Lady Cecily," he gave her a credible bow, his bright eyes crinkled in a smile. "You've grown up since last we met. I hardly recognized you."

"Everything and everyone changes eventually, Kendall." Long stared into Matt's face even though he spoke to his friend. "Matt has never quite understood why we mortals can't always stay as he wants us to be."

His idealism wasn't so great it couldn't be nudged aside by Long's continued harping! "Not again, Long! I want to hear no more about my being a martyr or a saint! In—"

"Stop bickering as if you were still schoolboys." Matt's blistering rebuttal was interrupted by his mother's firm words. "Matthew, you are about to become betrothed. And you, Richard, are as you've always been: a rational to the end."

Identical chocolate eyes met and clashed. "I cut my milk teeth on that philosophy, Mother."

"Of that, I am aware, my darling. Now, however, I must break up this fascinating gathering of minds. First, His Grace must be awakened for the party; the journey was hard on him. Cecily, a maid will bring supper to your room. And, gentlemen, I will see you downstairs in fifteen minutes, promptly." With Cecily in tow, his mother floated out of the room, her apparent delicacy belied by her adept management of them all.

"I'm going down to start imbibing immediately so I'll be completely cast away by the time your engagement is announced. Perhaps then I can stomach it." Shaking his head, Long turned on his heels.

"Wait for me, Longford. I'll march into the fray with you," Kendall offered, throwing Matt a jaunty salute.

"Aye, I can see we're all in for rare times ahead, laddie. The good Lord help us," Jeffries mumbled, leaving Matt alone.

Whereas a moment before, the room had been filled with everyone he held dear, except for his father and Serena, now solitude pressed in on him. Doubts! He had none. He was a man who knew what he wanted, and once he found it, wasted no time in securing it. He had always wished to be a soldier, and he was a damn good one. He had dreamed of the ideal woman, who embodied a sweet innocence which touched his heart. He had found her. In a week he would realize his dream and make Serena his bride.

· · ·

"It all seems like some wonderful dream, doesn't it, Serena? I'm quite flown away with success, I must tell you," Aunt Lavinia twittered, fanning herself beside the mirror as the maid buttoned Serena into her wedding dress. It was the dress of her dreams, the finest of white batiste with a demi train edged in embroidery. Her lace veil and matching gloves lay across the bed.

"You really are quite beautiful, Serena. I wonder why I never noticed before?" Aunt Lavinia questioned, her bulgy eyes studying Serena intently. "Although one could wish you would let a bit more bosom show. Oh, well, it doesn't matter now. The success of the Season is at our fingertips. We must simply enjoy it to the fullest!" Her lilac satin gown swishing about her, Aunt Lavinia moved across the room. "We leave for the church in an hour. To think Prinny will be in attendance! I must check to see your father has ordered the carriage. We mustn't be late."

Serena hove a sigh of relief at her exit. She needed a moment to herself—for the last week, she'd been feted and courted by the *ton* to the extent that she actually longed for the peace at the parsonage.

The maid finally succeeded in placing every ringlet just so and reached for the white roses Blackwood had sent. Cleverly twisting them into a simple cornet, she positioned them on Serena's head. But the fastening was proving difficult. Suddenly Serena's skull was nearly pierced by a sharp jab.

Her grimace of pain brought such a frightened look of horror to the maid's pinched little face, Serena smiled encouragingly.

"Don't be concerned. I'm quite all right. You've done such a lovely job—there's no need for haste. I believe the bride must be in attendance for the wedding ceremony to take place."

Her attempt at calming the little maid fell lamentably flat, for tears filled her pale brown eyes, and her fingers trembled as she worked again amidst the curls.

Racking her brain at how best to alleviate this poor child's fears, Serena hardly noticed the knock on the door. In the mirror she saw it open and a large woman enveloped in a brown traveling dress entered.

"Buckle!" Serena screamed, twisting around to throw

herself against the ample bosom of her old nursemaid, now rectory housekeeper. "The best, most wonderful surprise! However did you get here?" she asked, tearing herself out of Buckle's arms to gaze into her dear face.

She hadn't changed a whit! Her cheeks still reminded Serena of rosy apples, and the huge white coil of hair hung precariously, as it always had, at the back of her head. "When did dear Papa send for you? How thoughtful of him!"

"Dear child, it wasn't your papa, although I'm sure he would have had he thought of it. It was Lord Blackwood. He sent his own carriage to fetch me, with a note saying you told him there were three things you missed. He'd gotten you your garden and your papa, but needed me to fulfill all your dreams." Buckle's tiny rosebud mouth curled up in a smile of singular sweetness, which caused twinkles of light in her watery blue eyes. "He seems just the kind of man I've always dreamed for you."

Lord Blackwood. Somewhere in the whirl of activity the last week, he'd nearly gotten lost. It wasn't that she hadn't been with him every evening at routs, balls, and soirees, but that they were constantly surrounded by well-wishers. Serena's days had been so completely taken up with putting together a suitable trousseau, they'd had no time together.

As if someone suddenly walked into the room and emptied an ice-cold bucket of water over her head, ruining her coiffure and her wedding gown, she couldn't be more shocked. Suddenly she was awake to the fact she was marrying a stranger. She knew nothing of his thoughts. His kindness to Buckle was as surprising to her as it was touching.

The only thing she knew was when she looked at Blackwood, she was filled with quite shocking feelings which were frightening and exciting in the same instant.

"Lord Blackwood is very handsome, Buckle. And obviously from his kindness to you, just as handsome inside." Serena forced a smile, feeling somewhat better. "Now you are here, everything is perfect! Rest while I finish."

Only after settling dear Buckle in a chair did Serena look up and notice the maid still holding the white roses in her hands.

"Thank you, but you may go now. Mrs. Buckle will help me finish."

A hasty curtsy and a rapid exit showed how grateful the maid was not to have to put the finishing touches on Serena's wedding attire. Everyone seemed to be on tenter hooks about these nuptials. Truth to tell, it was just beginning to sink in that perhaps Papa was correct—this whirlwind courtship and wedding were a bit unorthodox.

"Buckle, no one does my hair as well as you. Please." She offered the roses to Buckle. Spreading her dress out around her, Serena slipped onto a low stool next to the chair. It brought back fond memories of the rectory and her childhood sitting like this before Buckle, and in a trice having her ribbons and flowers perfectly settled among her curls.

"There! It's perfect. You look lovely today, dear child," Buckle sighed, dropping her hands so Serena could clasp them fondly.

"Buckle, it's so wonderful you are here. Things have been happening so quickly, I've been at sixes and sevens. The city is such a wondrous place. There's an excitement in the air which gets inside one's blood and does the oddest things to normally sensible persons."

"And who might that just be, I wonder," Buckle teased, her rosebud mouth curling deeper at the corners. "I was afraid the city might frighten you—you being so sheltered and living such a simple country life."

Serena lowered her eyes, studying the sturdy brown cloth of Buckle's skirt. "I have something quite shocking to confess to you. You know Papa dislikes the city, so never speaks of it. And ... Aunt Lavinia, well ... you know Aunt Lavinia." She shrugged, finally finding the courage to meet Buckle's steady gaze. "The short of it, dear Buckle, is I would have been utterly terrified if a package hadn't arrived from the squire's niece six weeks before I left. That in itself was surprising, since I hadn't met with her after her travels abroad, but the note said the books were a gift from London for my kindnesses to her. Which I recall were nothing more than nudging her awake a few times during Papa's sermons."

Buckle stifled a chuckle, her apple red cheeks glowing. "Did you enjoy the books, dear child?"

"They were novels!" Serena was unable to restrain her own gurgle of laughter. "Quite shocking stories about life in the city. They were much truer than my imagination. I hadn't a clue how to go on until I read them."

"Well, how could you know!" Buckle snorted. "You with no mother, rest her soul, stuck away in the wilds of York in a tiny village. And the squire not doing his duty, only inviting you to the manor once a year on Boxing Day. And the present baron's wife too busy with her own children to have time for you. And your aunt only writing twice a year on your birthday and Christmas—sending gifts more suitable to a child than a growing woman. And me not a lady, so never having a Season. And your sainted papa so unworldly, he never thought what needed to be done to prepare you for the temptations of the *ton*. What was I to do?"

The new, rare, insight she'd first experienced with Lord Blackwood brought Serena to her feet. "Buckle, you sent me the novels?"

Bustling up, the former nursemaid fussed with Serena's dress as she'd done for years. "Well, not precisely. I asked my cousin, Miss Dunnforth, who lives here in the city, to send them. I added the note." As she peered up through short gray lashes, twinkling lights filled Buckle's eyes. "It would cause a scandal the length and breadth of Market Weighton if I'm found out. Shall we keep this our secret?"

Such a rush of affection overwhelmed her that, disregarding her elegant gown, Serena cast herself into Buckle's arms. "I love you!"

Laughing, she pressed a kiss on Serena's cheek before stepping back. "And I, you. But no more foolishness. We must be ready to leave for the church. Now, are we ready?" Squinting, she fussed at the flowers, tugged ever so gently upon the neckline of the gown, and settled the gossamer veil over all. Then she nodded, apparently satisfied.

"All is in order. Except one thing I must ask." The apple

cheeks shone bright red. "Has your Aunt Lavinia spoken to you about tonight with your husband?"

Serena turned to hide her own embarrassment by fussing with her long gloves. "Aunt Lavinia was vague at best. So was Papa, but I've grown up in the country. Joe, the stableboy, and I found the barn cats mating one afternoon. Poor Joe! I thought he'd have an apoplexy the parson's daughter had witnessed such a thing."

Buckle sputtered, "Dear child, I'm sure Lord Blackwood wouldn't like to be compared to a tomcat."

In all truth, Serena's feelings about what would happen on this, her wedding night, were as vague and unformed as had been the novels after the hero slammed the bedroom door shut behind him and his bride. But she must do something to soothe the alarming frown on Buckle's usually placid countenance.

"I'm sure Lord Blackwood will be as kind in his duties as husband as he has been in his dealing with me thus far. He has been all that is proper and noble." To her relief, the words accomplished their purpose; the rosebud mouth fell into its customary sweet lines.

"Obviously, dear child, in your short time together, you have come to know his lordship well."

"Yes and no, Buckle." Nervous flutters overcoming her, Serena laughed, dancing away for one last look in the mirror. "No time to waste!" Picking up the train of her gown, Serena went toward the door, Buckle following. "I don't wish to be late to marry the man of my dreams. And regardless of all else, that he truly is."

From the moment she and Lord Blackwood, truly magnificent in full military dress, stood before her father for the wedding service, through the chaste kiss on the lips before gliding hand in hand down the aisle as man and wife, onward to the wedding luncheon with its endless flow of champagne, food, and well-wishers, Serena moved as if in a romantic dream. It was magical and all was perfection.

Reality didn't intrude until Blackwood's dainty sister, Cecily, whispered in her ear that Her Grace, the Duchess of Avalon, and Mrs. Buckle were waiting in the west wing suite, which had been prepared for her wedding night. She excused herself to Blackwood, and his eyes gazed at her with such intensity that, suddenly, her thoughts of this night were not so vague.

Nervous flutters threatened to completely overwhelm her when she found the duchess and Buckle laying out a lacy negligee and gown. She stopped dead in her tracks, until the duchess took her hands, warming them with her own sure clasp.

"I know you are nervous, Serena, which is why I asked Mrs. Buckle to help you retire instead of one of our maids. I'm only here to tell you how pleased I am Matthew has chosen so well." Cupping Serena's cheeks with graceful fingers, she studied her face, then kissed her once. "I am delighted to have such a beautiful new daughter."

Serena still couldn't move even after Her Grace floated away in a cloud of silver chiffon.

"Her Grace is a true lady. And the little Cecily, she's a right sweet one. Dear child, it's a wonderful family you have now."

Buckle's voice drew her to the mirror, where she stood quietly allowing her to remove the flowers from her hair and slip off her satin pumps.

"I'm married, Buckle."

In a matter of minutes Serena was wearing the sheer layer of lace and the negligee.

"Let me brush your hair, dear child," Buckle soothed, pulling the brush carefully through her thick curls.

Serena sat on a slipper chair before the fire and gazed into the flames, trying to settle the shudders waving through her body. Blackwood would sweep her up in his arms and then … what?

Twisting around, she stared into Buckle's face, shadowed by the flickering flame. "Buckle, I've experienced such strange feelings since arriving in London. It's almost as if I'm becoming a different person."

"Not a different person, dear child. You're simply growing up, as I knew you would." Buckle gave her a comforting hug. "You're my little kitten who has always been warm and cared for in her small wicker basket. Then one day she discovers she can climb out and find a whole new world full of danger and excitement and joy. But the basket is always there to climb back into, dear child. Be happy," she whispered through what sounded suspiciously like tears, but Serena couldn't be sure, for Buckle whirled away, leaving the room too quickly.

She sat alone before the fire waiting for her husband. Lord Matthew Blackwood. A man she'd known a scant few weeks. A man who with one look caused her to act not by logic, but emotion.

The flutters turned to coils of excitement, forcing her up and around the room. She noticed the welcoming touches the duchess had provided—silver brushes and combs with her new initials engraved on them, a small posy by her lamp, and a miniature of Matthew, age eleven. She studied it for a moment, then restlessly moved to the window. The streetlamps were glowing, all in a row, like small moons in the darkness of Mayfair.

Finally she faced the huge bed with its crimson velvet hangings and sheets that smelled of lavender and sunshine.

Then she heard stirrings on the other side of the door leading to Blackwood's dressing room. In a panic, she dropped her negligee upon the chair and crawled into bed. Lying back against the plump pillows, she pulled the sheet high around her throat.

He found her there a moment later when he quietly entered, closing the door behind him. He cast one long look at her in bed and she held his rich chocolate gaze as long as she could. Then he slowly extinguished each candle until the bedchamber was lit only by firelight. She closed her eyes when she saw he was untying the sash of his robe. The bed gave with his weight and she felt his warmth slide along the length of her body.

"Open your eyes, sweetheart. I'm safely under the covers."

Dutifully she lifted her lids and found his whimsical smile only inches away beside her on the pillow.

"Have I thanked you for sending for dear Buckle?" She found, to her surprise, her voice sounded oddly husky.

"Several times." The corners of his mouth deepened. "I

wanted everything to be perfect for my bride."

"Why did you wish me for your bride, Blackwood?" she asked, her heart doing an odd little catch as she stared into those mesmerizing eyes.

He shifted closer and reached a hand to arrange her hair in a proper fall across the pillow. "I wanted you for my bride because I love you, sweetheart. Surely you must know that."

But what could he love? He didn't even know she wasn't a good horsewoman, but an excellent gardener. Had he discovered she was utterly devoted to Papa and Buckle, and even Aunt Lavinia in her own fashion? Is that what he admired, her strong familial feelings? Was it her scholarship? She knew little about the world, but she'd memorized the texts of almost as many sermons as her father. Was it her way with the parish children? He knew so little about her, what could he admire? It was suddenly vitally important to know.

"What do you love about me?" The huskiness caused her to whisper.

A thrill of enticing fear shook her as he brushed each of her eyelids with his lips.

"I love the goodness shining out of your eyes," he whispered. He trailed a finger down her cheek. "I love your perfect nose."

A shy rapture made her heart pound against her ribs as his finger traced her mouth.

"I love the very proper words coming out of these cherry lips. I love the way you chew just here when you're considering the proper way of things."

Suddenly the tip of his tongue replaced his finger on her often-abused lower lip. "Quite simply, Serena, I love everything about you."

"I believe"—her voice shook slightly—"that is enough for now."

Finally their lips met, and sweetly they tasted one another. Shifting his arm, he eased her closer so her body came in contact with every inch of his. Without words he held her until her tense limbs slowly yielded. Only then did he continue brushing her lips in feathery kisses which left her wishing for deeper contact.

With a sigh he acquiesced, his lips parting hers, tenderly probing, filling her with exquisite longings hitherto unknown.

Like a wonderful dream, she could do naught but flow with his magic and follow his tender encouragements. Wrapped in his arms, suffused with new, exquisite sensations, at last, she fell asleep.

When the embers in the fireplace were nothing but a faint glow in the darkness he reached for her again. Joyfully she went into his arms.

If the books Buckle had provided and the excitement of London had stirred new emotions in Serena, Blackwood carried her to a magical place where the contentment of her past life became a pale, faded image. Contentedly resting her cheek against his warm bare chest, she almost forced her weighted lids open at hearing an unfamiliar voice, but Blackwood reassured her with a quiet whisper. So she sank deeper into him, refusing to wake from her dream. She was safe now. Nothing, ever, could take this away from her.

The Separation

1813

Sometime during the night they shifted position: Serena was no longer resting her cheek against Blackwood's chest, nor could she hear the strong, even beats of his heart. But she could hear his voice repeating her name over and over again. To respond she must brush aside the cobwebs of sleep and open her eyes.

He was sitting beside her on the edge of the bed; but with a jolt that brought her fully awake, she realized he was already in traveling clothes.

"Oh, no, I've overslept! You're ready to leave for our bridal trip to Avalon Landing." Struggling up from the pillows, she pushed strands of loose curls off her face. "I shall be ready in a trice, I promise."

"Sweetheart, I have bad news." His now familiar and dear whimsical smile didn't quite reach his dark eyes. "Orders arrived unexpectedly last night from the War Office. I must return to my regiment immediately."

Still dazed with sleep, it took a few seconds for the full impact of his words to sink in. "You are leaving now?" The question came out in a breathless little whisper. Last night she had with eager hands let go of the past to joyfully embrace the future; now it was ending with hardly more than a beginning.

Biting her lower lip, she felt tears wash her eyes— Blackwood's stricken face wavered through a watery haze.

"Sweetheart!" He crushed her against his chest, holding her in the strong arms she'd so very recently come to know. "I'm sorry about the Landing. You'd love it there! But I must return to my duties."

Rubbing her cheek against the rough wool of his jacket, she gave a small hiccup. "I know. But I thought we'd have time to become better acquainted, as we started to last night. I was quite looking forward to it."

"The things you say," he chuckled into her ear, placing a kiss there. "I wished the same, sweetheart. But it's not to be." Shifting long fingers through her curls, he settled them around her throat and with gentle thumbs tilted her face up so she was gazing into his face, his eyes deep and fathomless.

"Remember, I leave my heart here in your keeping."

"And you take mine with you," she whispered, trembling with the emotions his words evoked. She closed her eyes and swayed against him. With a sigh of relief she felt his lips press hers and she clung to him as if she could not get close enough. Her lips burned against his, urgently wanting to leave a mark there so she could not be forgotten in the months ahead.

He pulled away first to cup her tearstained face with long fingers, his mesmerizing eyes searching her every feature. "I want to remember you just as you are now. Sweet, perfect Serena. Promise me you'll never change. That when we're reunited everything will be just as it is at this moment."

"I promise." At this moment she would promise to tether him the moon if he wished it.

In response, his lips scorched the tender skin on the side of her neck. Her hands clung weakly to him as his lips worked their way gently from her ear, down her jawline, until at last they touched her mouth. She drank in his deep kiss to store this sweetness within so it would always be a part of her.

He lifted his lips to taste her salty, tear-brimmed lashes. "Don't open your eyes," he commanded. With gentle hands he eased her back down upon the pillows and she felt him brush a curl off her face. "Go back to sleep, sweetheart, and dream of my return."

She did as she was bid, clutching at the top of the sheet with trembling fingers and swallowing down sobs. She felt the bed lift with the removal of his weight, and heard the door click shut behind him. Even then she didn't open her eyes. Her new happiness had been so short-lived, now replaced by a curious sense of impending tragedy. At the back of her mind she'd known Blackwood would return to war, but it had seemed a distant separation. For the whirlwind days of their courtship, so full of romance and burgeoning emotion, it had been easily disregarded. Now the sheer weight of loss—of something so new and so slightly explored, when she instinctively knew its depths held delight and fulfillment-caused her saddened mind to seek solace in the oblivion of slumber.

She awakened to sunlight streaming through narrow breaks in the heavy curtains. For two deep breaths she was disoriented. The crimson velvet draping the large bed was so vastly different from her narrow cot at home in the rectory. Now this opulent room with the rich hues of an oriental carpet and the fine carved wooden furniture was home. Her home with Blackwood. It seemed but a dream, all of it, but her body told her differently. Last night in Blackwood's arms had been real.

Hugging herself, she sat up, her eyes feeling puffy and weighted from her bout of weeping. Tears would wash nothing away. Blackwood had returned to his duty as a soldier, and in truth, she must accept it, for she valued his honor as much as his love. She must now, alone, take up her duty as his wife.

A soft knock sounded at the door before it was opened. Instead of a maid, Cecily entered carrying a silver tray with a pot, two cups, and a rack of toast.

"Good morning, Serena. I hope you don't mind I've come to share your breakfast of chocolate and toast."

Placing the tray carefully on the bed, Cecily eased down beside it. The deep brown eyes were so like Blackwood's, fresh pain tightened Serena's throat.

"Thank you, Cecily. I'm afraid I'm not fit company this morning."

"I understand." A small hand patted Serena's bare arm. "It's of all things unfair. That stupid War Office! Tearing a groom from the bosom of his bride on their wedding night. It's monstrous!"

This being Serena's first glimpse of Cecily's flair for the

dramatic, she couldn't help smiling in spite of her sadness. "I appreciate your sentiments. But Blackwood must do his duty."

"Matt always does his duty. He's the most honorable of men. And quite dashing and handsome. Both my brothers are brilliant catches, I'm told. I'll confess my friends all either have a tendre for Matt or Long."

Serena's only contact with the marquess had been at official social engagements, where he seemed to do nothing but glare at her through hooded eyes weighed down by heavy black lashes. She suspected he might hold a certain appeal for some women since his rakish appearance did bear strong resemblance to the heroes in the novels she'd read, but he frightened her.

"I probably shouldn't be confessing such things to you," Cecily laughed, pouring them each a cup of steaming hot chocolate. "But you have no need for concern. Matt fell in love with you at first sight and swept you off your feet. It's the most romantic thing I've ever seen! Gossip says you're the envy of the Season. Never before has anyone had a come-out ball one month and a wedding the next. I plan to do the same, of course." With a smug smile, Cecily bit into a piece of toast.

The warm, soothing chocolate eased Serena's tight throat. "Your come-out isn't until next Season, is it not? It's difficult to predict how one will react. I could never have predicted what has transpired between Blackwood and me." Although there was barely a year difference in age, after last night, Serena felt much older and wiser.

"I know exactly how it will be." Cecily nodded, her dark eyes sparkling above rose-flushed cheeks. "I've known since I was fourteen. I'm going to wed Lord Kendall."

"Kendall!" Serena gasped, remembering Blackwood's friend with the crisp, sandy curls and laughing green eyes.

"Can you keep a secret, Serena?" Cecily asked in awesome seriousness, leaning slightly forward.

Since she had never had brothers and sisters, the intimacy of shared confidences was foreign to her, but such was the appeal of Cecily's little heart-shaped face, Serena learned toward her eagerly. "Of course I can keep a secret."

"Lord Kendall has already kissed me. Twice!"

As mature as Serena felt after last night, her strict upbringing brought her bolt upright in shocked indignation. "But how dare he? And how could he face Blackwood after such a dastardly deed? You're just a child!"

Serena could tell by the sudden narrowing of Cecily's eyes she didn't care to be called a child, but she shrugged good-naturedly. "No doubt he doesn't even recall the incident. I was fourteen and Long came home to Avalon Hall in Berkshire to rusticate. Matt and Kendall were down from Oxford for a fortnight holiday. One night they were all drunk as monks in the library. I crept down to take a look. Matt and Long were both passed out on the couches. But Kendall, sprawled in a wing chair, was still awake. He saw me and called me to him." A faraway look came to Cecily's fine brown eyes. "He pulled on my braid and asked what I did there. I told him I'd come to see my brothers. 'Cast away the lot of them,' he said with that wonderful laugh of his which makes green devils dance in his eyes. He said I must retreat to my bedchamber before I was caught by Nannie. But before he sent me away, he kissed me on both cheeks."

Serena was aware of intense relief, for she'd liked Lord Kendall and was happy to find she could continue to do so.

"I fell in love with him then and there, and have remained constant. All I must do is go through the form of a Season and I shall be free to marry him. It's a romantic lot you've married into, Serena." Cecily laughed, and the light, musical sound was like a balm to Serena's bruised spirit. "Except Long and Mother, of course. Speaking of which, I nearly forgot!" With a little bounce, Cecily rose from the bed. "Mother is waiting in the front parlor. I believe she wants to show you around the town house and introduce you to the staff."

When Cecily entered the room, Serena was at the point of becoming a watering pot; now she was suffused with fresh energy.

"Cecily, did someone send you up here to lift my spirits?" Hugging her knees, Serena smiled at her new sister. "In truth, you've done just that!"

"Good!" Cecily nodded, a dimple appearing in her cheek,

instead of marking her chin as Blackwood's did. "Mother said it might help if you talked to someone closer to your own age. Mother may not be romantic, but you'll find her very wise."

Truly Serena appreciated the Duchess of Avalon's gentle wisdom as she introduced her to her new duties. Since Blackwood and she had discussed virtually nothing, she was surprised to learn the west wing of the town house was Blackwood's, the east Longford's, when the entire family was in residence. The family seat, Avalon Hall, in Berkshire comprised fifteen hundred acres and two towns. Blackwood's main seat was Avalon Landing on the Sussex Coast, a large, sprawling place he loved but had spent little time at, so it was in the hands of an estate manager, Mr. Jeremy Stockton.

Longford, as heir, had two minor estates in his care, for one day Avalon Hall would be his. Along with these facts, the duchess imparted a myriad details concerning the running of such a large establishment as the London house. Although, she confessed with her light, musical laugh, this household was small compared to the other holdings.

Truly overwhelming for a parson's daughter, but Serena found the training Buckle had provided stood her in good stead. Her mind was so cluttered with facts and names and lists, the jolting pain of Blackwood's abrupt departure began to fade ever so slightly. She guessed the duchess was wise enough to keep her busy so she wouldn't grieve.

Blackwood had been gone less than a fortnight when they were interrupted in the conservatory by Wilkens, who, with a pained expression in his small eyes, looked down his long, imposing nose at the shorter man beside him.

"This gentleman has come with a message from Lord Blackwood for Lady Serena. He insisted my lord said he must give it in person."

"That he did!" The thin man, dressed in rough country clothes, nodded enthusiastically. "Gave my word, Harry Thurston did, and keepin' it I am."

Rising to her feet, Serena stepped toward where he stood clutching a large clay pot of greenery.

"Is this for me, sir?" Even as he nodded, she took the pot in her hands. "This is a chrysanthemum plant, is it not?"

"Aye, my lady. Lord Blackwood, he was passing by, for our cottage is near the sea, and spied my wife tending the garden. A generous man, my lord. Says I'm to bring this planting and this here note."

Carefully setting the pot on the wide rim of the central fountain whose shepherdess eternally poured water from a pail onto the stones around her feet, she reached for the small piece of paper he thrust toward her.

"Sweetheart, I'm reliably informed these red chrysanthemums are symbolic of true love. Think of me as you tend this symbol of my deep, abiding affection. Blackwood."

Embarrassment burned her skin, scorching her throat as she realized she'd spoken the intimate words aloud. Stricken, she stared from Mr. Thurston, who continued to nod enthusiastically, to Wilkens, whose stern demeanor suddenly blurred a bit around the edges.

"Very thoughtful. Thank you, Mr. Thurston." The duchess's musical voice bridged the awkward moment. "Wilkens, see that Mr. Thurston has ample food and drink for his journey home."

The men retired from the scene while the duchess tactfully admired the plant, giving Serena a moment to recover.

"Will it bear blossoms? I fear horticulture is not a particular interest of mine."

"Yes, Your Grace, in autumn there will be lovely red blooms which will return year after year if attended properly," she finally managed.

"Perhaps we should turn it over to the gardener for care."

"Oh, no, Your Grace! I shall attend it myself," Serena put in hurriedly. "Gardening is an interest of mine."

As if Serena had said something that pleased her greatly, the duchess gave her a deep, warm smile. "I'm delighted to hear it. I have something else which I hope will interest you." She lifted a slim volume from a small marble table nearby. "This is Matthew's favorite book of poetry. Perhaps reading what has given him pleasure will bring you closer to him. But now, I fear,

I must attend His Grace—this is our reading hour."

Left with Blackwood's book of poetry and his gift, Serena carefully chose the best spot in the conservatory for the plant. She felt the soil, added more water, and removed two yellow leaves. It was strangely reassuring to have some tangible evidence of Blackwood's regard, for their time together did seem dreamlike, almost a figment of the romantic nature that had blossomed within her so recently.

In reality she had new responsibilities and challenges which excited her as nothing had before. Perhaps dear Buckle was right, she was like a kitten curious and eager to explore her new world and discover all its mysteries and delights.

She clutched the volume of poetry to her breast. If this was his favorite, then it would be hers, too. Blackwood had touched something within her she'd never dreamed existed. Was it quite proper to feel as she had on their wedding night? She blushed now remembering it. Whatever the quality he possessed that made her instinctively trust him had been reinforced by all she'd learned in the last few days about the kind of man he was. With insight that was no longer so rare, she recognized how fortunate she was in that discovery.

She stayed reading in bed until the candles sputtered. Even when she closed her eyes, the lines of poetry danced across her lids. Her vision of Blackwood as her romantic hero filled her dreams.

Over the next few weeks the duchess presented her with more books that she said Matthew had enjoyed. As Serena read them, a picture of her husband's true personality began to take form. It began to give substance to the dreamlike figure he always appeared to her, taking him out of the realm of larger-than-life and into every small detail of her days.

The Season continued its feverish pursuit around them, but the Avalons refused more invitations than they accepted. Often the four of them, Serena, Cecily, and Their Graces, would spend a quiet evening at home playing whist. Blackwood's father was not well, his ashen color showing a weakness of the heart the Prince Regent's physician himself shook his head over.

With kind thoughtfulness all Blackwood's family made her feel welcome, all but Longford. His apparent disdain was a constant, albeit slight, mar on her new life.

There was no disdain on the marquess's face the night he burst into the library, where she and Cecily sat reading Shakespeare aloud.

"Where is Father?" he demanded sharply.

Fear gripped Serena, holding her perfectly still; but Cecily sprang to her feet.

"Long, what is it?" she asked with a frightened little catch in her voice.

"Dispatches have arrived about a great victory at Vitoria. Matt is well or we would have heard."

"And Kendall?" The wide eyes stared intently at her brother, pleading for reassurance.

"Well, brat! Now fetch Mother so I might inform her."

Picking up the hem of her dress, Cecily nearly flew from the room.

Serena's numbing fear evaporated with Longford's words, and relief wrenched a sob from her lips. Blackwood was safe. There had been no letter since the cherished chrysanthemum plant. Although she knew mail from the Peninsula was slow, and often as not, unreliable, her fear had grown to almost unbearable proportions. The rest of them were so cheerful and optimistic, she'd been afraid to voice her concern. Now tears of relief flowed down her cheeks.

"Good God, stop your blubbering and grow up! I was hoping Her Grace would put some bronze on you and change you into a woman worthy of my brother." Longford sneered, even as he proffered a handkerchief.

She refused it, leaping to her feet, confusion and anger warring within her. "How dare you? Your brother holds me in deep affection just as I am and wishes me never to change!"

"You're both babes in the woods!" Leaning one broad shoulder against a convenient prop, he studied her with mocking, hooded eyes. "Matt hasn't the slightest idea what, if anything, lies behind your pretty face. He only sees what he wants to see.

He embodies all of us with the qualities he wishes us to possess. Someday he'll be forced to accept the world, and us, as we are, warts and all. I suggest it's in your best interest to become the kind of woman up to the challenge that will present. Quite frankly, I doubt you have it in you."

His mocking contempt on the heels of her fear and relief caused her to clasp trembling fingers over her quivering lips. Bolting from the room, she fled past a stunned Cecily and the duchess, instinct leading her to the only tangible symbol of the regard Longford held in such contempt.

Moonlight bathed the conservatory, where the chrysanthemum flourished under her expert care. She sat beside it, letting her tears of relief flow where none could see. There were so many new emotions bursting inside her, she could hardly contain them. Especially her feelings for Blackwood, which were growing stronger as she slowly began to know him through his family and friends. Even his belongings gave clues to his character. With a jolt of anger she admitted Longford was correct in his assumption she was totally devoid of town bronze, just as she'd been totally unprepared for Blackwood's whirlwind courtship. But something inside her had risen to both the challenge of her Season and Blackwood's affection. And that something wouldn't let her down now.

She'd learned so much about herself in the months since her wedding. She'd thought she was fairly well educated, for a female, until Her Grace, a renowned bluestocking, took her under her wing. If the forbidden novels had exposed Serena's latent romantic nature, the books the duchess gave her opened new doors to history and politics, to social reform, and a whole world of ideas. Yet everything the duchess exposed her to had some bearing on Blackwood or the things he loved, especially Avalon Landing.

Slowly the decision formed to go to the Landing for the summer and autumn instead of to Avalon Hall with the rest of the family. There she could feel even closer to the man she'd known so briefly and wed. Blackwood loved the place; surely he would wish her to care for his holdings as she was the planting he'd sent. Running a gentle finger over the tight buds, she smiled, her decision providing a surge of self-confidence. Dear Buckle might say her kitten was discovering the claws necessary to expand her world. That thought was almost as disturbing as it was comforting.

When she informed the duke and duchess of her decision, they were most agreeable, insisting only that Longford accompany her for protection, and Cecily for companionship.

The duchess wore a most satisfied smile. When Serena inquired, Cecily had a ready reply.

"Mother has been hoping you'd take an interest in Avalon Landing."

Surprised, Serena shook her head. "Then why didn't she suggest it? I value her opinion."

"Mother never suggests. She simply leads you until you find the proper path yourself." The dimple deepened in her cheek. "It can be quite vexing, can't it? Never knowing quite what she wishes you to do. And Long is just like her! But you'll get used to it. We all have." Cecily gave her an impulsive hug. "We'll have such fun at the Landing, you'll see!"

Although delighted with the prospect of seeing her new home, Serena longed to hear from Blackwood. Anxiety for his safety and the outcome of each battle weighed heavily on her, but she dared not share these thoughts with his family, who all appeared so optimistic. Unfortunately, within a week the London house would be closed up. The delays in receiving a letter would be even greater in the country.

Finally, on the eve of departure, Wilkens presented the long-anticipated letter to her. It was soiled with travel and dog-eared, but it was thick. She fled with the treasure to her bedchamber and locked her door. Excitement threatened to overwhelm her. Slowly she opened the sheets of paper, and as she recognized his handwriting, her throat tightened with often-repressed tears.

> My dearest Serena, by now word of our glorious
> victory at Vitoria against Joseph Bonaparte has reached
> you. My men fought bravely and their valor has not

gone unrecognized. My Sergeant Major, Higgens, distinguished himself; a veteran of more campaigns than I have years, he is a source of much inspiration to the men and to me. Like Jeffries, he's a Scot and they often entertain us around the campfire. The men are full of confidence fired by the honor of our quest as we prepare to cross into France. Even the cooks are bursting with good spirit for our iron cooking kettles have been replaced by tin so their task is lighter. I give you the way of the small things which make up my day so you will know how I spend the time of our separation. Just as I know what makes up your days. I can see you reading in the library with Cecily and my mother. Or working on your needlepoint. And at night playing whist with my parents; they enjoy it so. Tell my mother Kendall sends his regards and appreciation for the packet of books she sent for our journey. It is a sight I thought never to see—Kendall reading a volume on philosophy! Give Poppet my love and tell her Kendall sends his regards. Tell my father all goes well and the Marquess thinks it'll be soon over. And Longford will be receiving a letter from me about the Landing. Also give mother my thanks for procuring Shelley's Declaration of Rights. By now, sweetheart, you must know she is immensely well read and a proponent of education for all. How she procured a work banned as seditious I can only wonder with awe. One passage has given me much thought: No man has a right to do an evil thing that good might come. The men here try so hard and are good soldiers, but we are far from home. Mostly my thoughts are with my perfect sweet Serena. Care for our plantings as you tend the dream of my return, just as I do. Memory of our brief time together burns bright in my heart and hastens my determination to return to you. Until then I am forever,

your Blackwood

She closed her eyes to picture him as she'd first seen him: a heroic figure stepping out of the pages of a novel. Now the fairy-tale hero was becoming a real person to her. The sweetness she'd sensed from the beginning, and the passion she'd learned on her wedding night, but there was so much more for her to discover. With a jolt of pain she yearned for him to return so she could continue the journey of discovery begun their wedding night.

Unbidden, tears filled her eyes and spilled down her cheeks. But they could change nothing, nor could these painful thoughts. For now, letters would have to do. She splashed cool water on her tight, hot face and tidied the cornflower blue ribbon in her hair before presenting herself to the family, generously sharing all of the letter, save the last passages for herself.

She stayed awake most of the night penning a long, detailed letter of everyday trivialities to Blackwood, along with her admiration for the bravery of his men and himself in their honorable war against Bonaparte's tyranny. In closing she told him how the chrysanthemum throve under her vigilance. Boldly she signed, "your devoted wife."

After sealing the letter, she tossed and turned on her bed for what remained of the night, memories of each of their few meetings making her restless. Near dawn she finally found a cool spot on the pillow for her hot cheek and drifted into light slumber.

Early in the morning, her eyes red-rimmed from sleeplessness, Serena directed a footman to bring her plant from the conservatory.

Longford looked up from his breakfast. "Good God, you're not bringing that thing with you!"

"Of course she is! It's so romantic, I can't bear it! Will it bloom soon, Serena?" Cecily asked eagerly, the morning sun through the ceiling-high windows highlighting her curls into white gold.

"Yes, in the autumn it will have beautiful red flowers."

"I shall stay with you until it blooms," Cecily declared, adjusting her crimson bonnet. "I only wish I had such a symbol of Lord Kendall's regard. Let's be off at once; I'm anxious to see the coast."

As the carriage rumbled by the last building in the outlying districts, Serena leaned forward to gaze back at London. Chimney smoke hung over it, obscuring the church spires and towers of the city. So much had happened to her there—a whole new world had opened to her. Yet she looked forward to being in the countryside again with clear blue sky overhead and fresh, bracing air. She took her role as Blackwood's wife seriously and anticipated the responsibilities. She would perform her duty with as much honor as he would expect—for surely a man who fought so bravely for his country would prize honor and duty above all else. Satisfied, she sat back in the coach and asked Cecily to describe Avalon Landing to her.

The Landing was essentially of Tudor design, but Blackwood's successive ancestors had added wings and turrets so now it sprawled, seemingly unendingly, on a slight rise in a parklike setting Serena found enchanting. Immediately she perceived a need for her gardening skills.

Warned of her arrival, the butler, Stevens—a second cousin to Wilkens, she discovered later, which no doubt accounted for their similarity—had assembled the staff. Serena was grateful for Longford's initial introduction to Stevens, who in turn made her known to everyone from the kitchen tweeny to the head groomsman.

"Mr. Stockton will see you in the estate office in the west wing at your convenience, my lady," Stevens informed her in a deep, mournful voice which was slightly disconcerting, since it reminded her so forcibly of Wilkens in London.

"I shall see him within the hour," she heard herself saying with a calmness she was far from feeling. "And could Mrs. Broxton provide us with some tea in the drawing room, please? I'm sure Cecily would like some refreshment."

Promptly an hour later, after making certain Cecily was settled comfortably on a cream daybed in the ladies' salon, Serena pushed open the doors to the office adjacent to the paneled library. To her shock, Longford was there, too, standing with his shoulder propped against a carved mantel. He was involved in an animated conversation with the cavernous-cheeked man who sat behind the dark walnut desk.

He rose to a truly remarkable height as she entered. "My lady, I am Mr. Jeremy Stockton, Lord Blackwood's estate manager for Avalon Landing. The estate records are all in order."

"I'm sure they are, Mr. Stockton. I shall examine them myself tomorrow." She moved forward and extended her hand, wishing to measure the man by the strength of his grasp. "I know we will deal extremely well together."

A short, harsh laugh from Longford raised her hackles. The duchess had spent several months teaching her the proper way of things, and she'd taken care of the rectory accounts for years, so felt utterly secure in her position. She turned what she hoped was a quelling look upon Longford's mocking face.

"I am quite accustomed to perusing account books, Longford. But I thank you for your concern." Giving him no time to respond, she spun around and departed with dignity.

The rest of the afternoon was spent exploring with Cecily, who proved to be an entertaining guide. Stories of Matt's exploits as a young man sent them both often into gales of laughter. His presence was apparent in every room and in the devotion of the staff. By the time she was finished, Serena understood why he loved the place so well.

Longford entered the estate office with Mr. Stockton when she completed her examination of the books. Obviously he was still uncertain of her ability. Having nothing to prove, to him or to herself, she pretended he wasn't there.

"Mr. Stockton, I notice expenditures five years ago for repairs to our tenant cottages, but nothing since."

"That's correct, my lady." His head bobbled in a nod at the top of his long, gangly neck. "His lordship wished to improve the dwellings."

She folded her hands in front of her, ignoring Longford to concentrate on Mr. Stockton's blank, pale face. "But what about maintenance?"

"In my opinion, my lady, the structures are sound as they are."

"I shall ride out and see for myself tomorrow. I'd like a

complete list of the tenants—family size, position on the estate, and so forth—with an appraisal of their productivity and perhaps a list of their needs before I go. When I return from my tour we shall discuss the matter again. Thank you, Mr. Stockton," she said with a dismissive smile which he quickly understood, departing with a long, loose stride.

Longford strolled out after him, but stopped in the doorway to ask, "What would Matt make of his country mouse now, I wonder?"

He left her with an enigmatic smile startlingly reminiscent of his mother.

As much as Serena tried to ignore it, a niggling worry frayed at her mind. She hadn't really changed. She was simply doing her duty as her father and Buckle had taught her and as Blackwood would surely wish. He loved the Landing. In his absence she would strive to make it all he would wish.

Cecily accompanied her in an open landau for the round of visits. They were greeted warmly by all, whose kind inquiries about her husband and praise for his management heartened her. It was obvious that Blackwood wished his tenants to be comfortable and happy. Young children played about some of the cottages; older boys could be seen helping their fathers. The estate seemed to be running smoothly, but her inquisitive eyes picked out thatched roofs and fences that needed repair before winter, and dwellings that could do with new whitewash.

At one home a young girl sat on a low bench in the yard with several even younger children clustered about her. Serena was astounded to see she was reading from a book in her lap. She ordered the driver to stop.

"Where could the child have learned to read?" she inquired of an equally mystified Cecily.

By this time the cottage door opened, a woman, obviously in an interesting condition, standing in the doorway. "Children," she commanded. Immediately they sprang forward to offer their curtsies and bows.

"I'm Mrs. Brown, my lady. Would you and Lady Cecily care for a cool drink?"

"That would be most kind, Mrs. Brown." Serena stepped out of the carriage and turned toward the eldest child. "And what would your name be?"

Shyly the girl looked up, still clutching the book as if it were precious. "Polly, my lady."

"You were reading to the younger children?"

The child blushed. "No, ma'am. Just tellin' stories to fit the pictures. The vicar's wife gave me the book."

Mrs. Brown bustled forward with two glasses of water. "My daughter's the clever one," she said proudly. "Mrs. Morton keeps saying she should learn her letters."

Serena smiled at the little group. "Perhaps one day I can come back and hear a story, too. Thank you for the drink, Mrs. Brown. Is there anything you or Mr. Brown need for the coming winter?"

"Thank you, your ladyship. We'll do just fine. Polly will help when the new babe comes."

Polly seemed young to have that kind of responsibility, but Serena didn't comment. On the way home in the landau she was silent, ordering her thoughts. As they reached the front door, abruptly she announced, "The vicar and his wife, the Mortons? They should come to tea directly."

She presented her list to Mr. Stockton the next morning. After only the briefest of hesitations, he bowed. "As you wish, my lady. I shall see to it immediately."

She waited until he left the room before collapsing into a deep wing chair in the library in thought. She'd once told Buckle she was fearful of the changes going on inside her. Could she have turned so completely from dutiful to demanding? What she required was necessary, though. If Blackwood were here, he would agree. Wouldn't he?

Leaping to her feet, she shook off such feelings. She was simply following the path Blackwood and the Duchess of Avalon opened before her.

That path would have been most idyllic were it not for her fears for Blackwood in the next weeks as she and Cecily explored the Sussex Coast. Longford came and went as he pleased, going often to London and returning with news from the Peninsula, which was more often than not frightening. Even more upsetting was the absence of a letter.

Longford did not intrude on their pursuits, but occasionally joined them at dinner, and once attended service in the village with them.

The evening Serena invited the Reverend Morton and his hopeful family for an informal supper, Longford thrilled the three sons by showing them his horseflesh. Serena and Mrs. Morton reached an immediate understanding, and thereafter she became a great ally and a pipeline to the village.

As the autumn wore on, Serena and Cecily continued their visits to the tenants. Twice Serena kept her promise and returned to the Browns to participate in the storytelling. She learned to go slow with changes, allowing the people some time to accept her ideas.

That no further letters from Blackwood arrived was a constant dull ache. All she did for the estate and its people made her feel closer to him, but she yearned for more. The two messages she had received were already dog-eared from her constant rereading. She got into the habit of keeping a journal, thinking perhaps she would send it to him so he could see how her days were full of happiness and work.

Cecily was true to her word, staying until the chrysanthemum plant bore deep red blooms.

On the morning of her departure she hugged Serena tightly, tears standing in the dark chocolate eyes. "I shall miss you so! But before you know it, you'll be at Avalon Hall for the holidays. Will you not be lonely without us?" she asked, with a frown marring her usual sunny countenance.

"Father and Buckle will arrive soon and stay until we journey together to Avalon Hall for Christmas. Besides, I still have decorating in the house and the redesigning of the gardens to complete."

Cecily's light, musical laughter caused Serena to smile. "Wait until Matt sees the wonderful changes you've made here. When next you write, please give him my love. And send my regards to

Lord Kendall," she added with a pert grin before disappearing into the carriage.

Serena looked up at Longford astride his stallion, waiting silently beside the carriage. He gave her that same enigmatic smile.

"You just might do." He drew on the reins. With a nod from him, the carriage pulled away, and Longford galloped ahead, leaving her waving until they were out of sight.

Even without Cecily's companionship, the days were full. The nights were hard. She filled them by reading volumes from Blackwood's library, but it was difficult to concentrate when most of her thoughts were focused on receiving some kind of word from or about her husband. Her husband ... with whom she'd spent but one night, but who became more and more important to her each day. There would be so much for them to share when he returned.

She was in the library reading one of the books on political philosophy when Stevens solemnly presented a packet brought by messenger from London.

Inside were two letters. Overjoyed, she opened them both at once and found one dated in midsummer and the other much later. She read the earliest first, learning of the battle of San Sebastian and Blackwood's pride in his men, particularly Sergeant Major Higgens. In his words she experienced the deep affection and admiration he felt for the older man. Again the letter was full of the small details of his days: how the men hated the use of case shot and how he missed Kendall, who had been promoted to his own regiment. He closed with loving words and a whimsical inquiry into the wellbeing of their plantings.

She determined to press a chrysanthemum bloom this very night and enclose it in her next letter, along with the pages of her journal.

As long as it had taken the one letter to arrive, the other must have come through with the dispatches, for it was dated only a few weeks before.

> My dear Serena, Long has written you have taken up
> the reins at Avalon Landing, making sweeping changes.

Sweetheart, I'm happy you love the Landing as I do, but don't concern yourself with duties more suited to Mr. Stockton. By all means decorate as you please, for it's your home and I wish you to be content there. But the responsibilities of the estate are too heavy for my sweet Serena. She should be happily engaged in pursuits which will keep the beautiful smile on her cherry lips. Thoughts of you ease this time of heavy fighting for our cause. Sergeant Major Higgens is my right arm and also my friend. I look forward to the two of you meeting. He is an older, larger version of Jeffries and often treats me with the same wry wit, but never in front of the men. He is of all things the best of our fine fighting men. Often I dream of our hours together, sweetheart. Every night I go to sleep to the vision of you on our final morning. I live to awaken you with a kiss that wipes out this long separation and all will again be as it was. Never change, Serena, for you are perfection. Yours forever,

Blackwood

Unbidden, tears trickled down her face. A deep, swelling pain burst to life in her chest, bringing a terrible realization. While she was adding weight and strength and substance to the glittering, shallow image of Blackwood, seeing him as he truly was beyond the handsome face and dashingly broad shoulders which had first attracted her, he still only saw her as the embodiment of his dreams.

Although surely he was still that to her, even more so, now she recognized his true worth. It wasn't that thoughts of him didn't still make her breathless and a trifle giddy; on the contrary, the yearning grew stronger each day for his return.

With sickening dread the thought came to her Longford might be correct: Blackwood saw people as he wished them to be, not as they truly were. Perhaps he would not feel the same about her when he must live with her day after day. She could not then continue to be only a romantic dream. She would become a real person with human frailties.

Totally rejecting such thoughts, she rushed to the conservatory and snipped a blossom. While it pressed between heavy volumes, she penned a letter to Blackwood. She refused to admit she wrote it exactly as she would have done months ago and that there was no longer any thought of enclosing the journal pages. She placed the pressed crimson petals between the sheets and folded them over carefully, lifting them for a fleeting moment to her lips.

True love surely would conquer all. If indeed what Blackwood felt for her was as real as what she now felt for him.

Society

1814

Serena received Blackwood's Christmas letter in late January at Avalon Hall, where the entire family plus Aunt Lavinia and her cousin Frederick were snowed in. Tempers were slightly on edge from their forced confinement, especially Cecily, who was having to gently fob off Frederick's adoration. Longford, who was deprived of riding his wild stallion on a daily basis, had little to do with the assemblage, preferring to spend most of his time with his father in the study. The letter's arrival was a welcome diversion, so, as was her habit, Serena shared most of it. She read Blackwood's regards to all the family, his glorious reports of his men's bravery, and of course, the mention of Kendall for a rapt Cecily.

The rest of the letter was hers alone: regret they couldn't be together for their first holiday; delight at receiving the chrysanthemum petals, which he kept close to his heart. These passages fed the feelings Blackwood had inspired in her heart since the first time she looked into his dark eyes.

That the messenger was able to get through from London heralded the clearing of the roads. Aunt Lavinia prepared for her leave-taking by closeting herself with Serena in the small parlor. From the hard glaze in the huge blue eyes, Serena feared a scolding was at hand.

"You've done so brilliantly! How could you fail to be increasing?" her aunt fretted, the owl eyes blinking rapidly. "I'd so hoped you'd be setting up Blackwood's nursery. I know how pleased Charlesworth's family was when I produced dear Frederick within the first two years of our marriage. Really,

Serena, you must understand how important it is to secure the succession."

As much as her aunt's harsh words hurt, Serena refused to give in to the uncharitable retort that dear Frederick was a disgraceful rip who'd been sent down from Oxford more times than Serena could recall. Besides that, his mother only kept his antics under control through the dire threat of cutting off his allowance. She couldn't imagine Their Graces being pleased if she produced such an offspring to add to their old and noble line.

Instead she forced a smile. "Aunt Lavinia, you know Blackwood and I had only one night together before he was called away. When he returns we shall have ample time to think of such matters."

"Serena, you are as unworldly as your father after all!" Stretching her eyes as wide as possible, which was a frightening sight indeed, Aunt Lavinia leaned closer. "Have you forgotten men are killing one another in that dreadful war! Blackwood may never return, and you have failed to produce his heir!"

Fear such as she'd never known gripped her heart. Blackwood's letters were so full of the glory and the honor of war, she hadn't really looked beyond the idealistic words. Aunt Lavinia was right for once!

To think she'd been fretting Blackwood might be disappointed to find her slightly changed when there was every chance they might never be able to fully explore their feelings for one another. For the first time Blackwood's passages concerning his men's valor and bravery took on their true meaning. These men were fighting for their lives despite any glorious protestations.

Immediately upon her aunt's rather protracted leave-taking, Serena pleaded a headache and retired to her bedchamber. The letter she penned to Blackwood this night was the truest to her heart. That he might notice the change in her didn't seem a whit important now compared to her need for him to know her feelings. How could she have remained so naive?

Suddenly the reports, sketchy as they were, and Longford's discussions with his father, took on a deeper significance. At last she recognized their fear for Blackwood was greater than she'd imagined, for it was based on fact. She spent hours poring over maps, trying to trace her husband's movements during the past year.

Her constant fear for him colored all her actions. Within a fortnight of her aunt's departure she left for the Landing, anxious to oversee the spring planting and the changes in the gardens she had so lovingly designed.

The Reverend and Mrs. Morton were only too willing to assist her more charitable designs. Many of the villagers had lost a man to the war. Serena felt they should receive extra help from the estate. She trusted the reverend to devise a scheme so that even the severely wounded could still have a useful place.

She proposed a school for the younger children, thinking of Polly, and offered a stipend for anyone who could teach letters and basic mathematics. Mrs. Morton suggested a notice be posted in the village.

The vicar's wife had also brought a list of special needs, including a Mrs. Watley, a widow, who had just learned her twin sons had been killed at the Battle of Orthez. Her small farm had been given to a family man, and she had nowhere to go and little to support herself with. Serena assured Mrs. Morton she would think of something quickly and have Stockton see to it.

Convinced that Blackwood would be proud of these accomplishments, she departed for York for a brief visit with her papa and Buckle with a slightly lighter heart.

When she arrived back in London to prepare for Cecily's Season, the seemingly endless trips to the modistes and milliners on Bond Street kept her occupied, but always her thoughts were with Blackwood. This time last year she had first looked up into those mesmerizing dark eyes and lost her heart.

News of Napoleon's abdication on April 6 must have flown across the Channel, as Cecily phrased it. There was much rejoicing in London. The duke insisted on coming down for a celebratory dinner, for surely his son would be returning forthwith.

A toast to His Majesty, poor sick man, and the Regent, was quickly followed by a tribute to Matthew. Cecily squeezed her fingers under the table and shot her a wide, dimpled smile. Serena knew what was utmost in her mind: Kendall would be home during her Season, and she would have her opportunity to snare him.

Uppermost in Serena's thoughts was the anticipation of seeing Blackwood and again recapturing the dizzy emotions of their wedding night, which had ever haunted her dreams.

Her euphoria continued gaining strength as word of the Treaty of Fountainbleu reached London and men were rumored to be already returning. This Season's frivolities surpassed all that had gone before. The *ton* was prepared to celebrate victory without end.

One afternoon at tea she and Cecily regaled the duchess with the newest hearsay concerning troop movements and talked of nothing but Kendall and Blackwood's triumphal return. Her Grace was smiling indulgently at Cecily's dramatic protestations that she intended to honor Kendall as a hero of the nation all her life when Longford suddenly burst through the door.

Serena took one look at his set face and knew something was very wrong.

"Richard, what a pleasant surprise." The duchess gracefully lifted her hand for his kiss. "I shall have another cup brought immediately."

"No, Mother, I fear I need something stronger!" He sprawled in a chair next to his sister. "This came through with the dispatches, and since I was visiting a friend at the War Office, I said I would deliver it myself."

Since the large packet was directed to Her Grace, the Duchess of Avalon, she opened it. Inside were several sheets of paper folded over with their names on them. The duchess handed two to Cecily.

She instantly opened both. "One's from Matt wishing me a successful Season and bidding me not to break too many hearts. The other is from Lord Kendall." Her voice was full of breathless excitement as her eyes scanned the page. "He sends his regards and regrets he cannot be in attendance for my come-out ball but asks for the first waltz upon his return." She clutched the sheet tightly to her breasts with such an enraptured expression on her lovely face, even her cynical brother's long mouth curved in something other than his usual sneer.

"What does Matt say in your letter, Mother?" Longford asked carefully. Serena experienced the strongest feeling he was waiting for something.

"He sends us his love and his hopes for his father's improved health." Her smile didn't quite reach the dark eyes she had bequeathed to all her children. "We have the best for last. Serena, there are several sheets addressed to you."

Almost reluctantly, Serena unfolded her letter. She didn't get beyond the first few lines. Cold disappointment froze her until she forced herself to blink away the ache behind her eyes.

She looked straight at Longford. "You knew, didn't you?"

"I guessed, knowing my brother." He shrugged.

"What? What is it!" Cecily demanded, jumping to her feet, the precious note from Kendall still clasped to her bosom.

"Blackwood is not returning. Fourteen thousand men are to go to the colonies, and he feels honorbound to go with his regiment. Kendall goes also."

Cecily fell back into the chair, her eyes filling with tears.

Needing to be alone, Serena rose and sent a fleeting smile in Her Grace's direction. "Please, excuse me." It came out a broken whisper and she fled the room before she lost her composure entirely.

The conservatory was a refuge—the chrysanthemum plant sat in its place of honor: green and alive, but dormant. Dropping down beside it, she spread the sheets across her lap and forced herself to reread the hated words.

> Dearest Serena, after your last letter which was so heartfelt, I hesitate to write these words, but must. Now that we have vanquished Bonaparte we must attend the war in America, which has been hampered by a deficit of experienced men. My regiment volunteered to a man. I must be with them. Sweetheart, understand it is my duty to accompany my men to Chesapeake Bay.

With these veterans of the Peninsula we shall rout the colonists in short order. Sergeant Major Higgens was retiring, for you must know he's much older than most, but he, too, stays on to lend his help to our cause. I cannot desert my men before our task is done. Most of Kendall's regiment also goes. Dearest Serena, understand I do what I must, but know full well I feel as you do and ache to be reunited. In your words I sense some changes in you, but I carry the perfect image of you in my heart and I cling to it. Tend carefully the symbol of our true love as I do each day we are parted.

Blackwood

He wasn't coming home! His love of duty obviously was more important than any feelings he had for her. While her regard for him had deepened, being surrounded by his things and the people who loved him most, had she become nothing more than a pleasant memory? Refusing to give in to such thoughts, she shut her eyes, reliving each of their meetings in her mind.

She only lifted her lids when she heard Cecily's whisper and felt her kneel beside her. She looked into the tear-streaked little face.

"Serena, they aren't coming. What if they never return?" Cecily asked with a sharp catch in her voice.

"Of course they shall return." From where came the even tone? "Blackwood says they shall rout the colonists in short order."

"Serena, my friend Mary Featherstone's brother, Sir Giles, never returned from the Peninsula. And there have been others." Her voice dropped to the merest whisper, her eyes filling her white face. "It could happen to Matt or Kendall."

"Cecily, I forbid you to speak so!" Serena retorted in stronger tones. No matter she ached inside as if a hole had been ripped through her. No one would ever see the despair she felt. She rose, pulling Cecily to her feet. "Both Blackwood and Kendall will return victorious, I have no doubts. Nor should you."

Cecily held on to her hands so tightly, they hurt, but Serena didn't pull away. "Serena, what shall we do?"

"Do?" She forced a laugh and was pleased to discover it sounded real. "Why, enjoy your Season, of course. They would both wish us to do so, and I fully intend to."

Those moments alone with the late afternoon sun bathing the conservatory in golden light forged a bond between the two girls. They never spoke of their fears again. Side by side they threw themselves into the most feverish pursuits of the Season. As all had predicted, Cecily was declared a diamond of the first water. Smitten beaus sent her poems describing her hair as cascading moonbeams and her eyes as pools of sweet chocolate. They smiled over the missives, but with her usual flair for the dramatic, Cecily refused to save any but Lord Kendall's brief note.

While Cecily left cracked hearts littering the *ton*, Serena formed a court of her own. Finally she learned the art of coy use of fan and lashes Aunt Lavinia labored so last Season to teach her. It was really quite simple when one's emotions were so uninvolved. Now it was merely a game they all played for one another's amusement.

When she heard herself termed a reigning beauty, she was so shocked, she hid her laughter behind her fan. What a change of fortunes for Miss Serena Fitzwater of Market Weighton, East Riding, York! What would Blackwood make of this creation that the *ton* was forming?

She tried not to dwell on thoughts of him. Although sometimes she would catch a glimpse of Longford—his shining hair or his dark eyes—so reminiscent of Blackwood that it seemed an arrow pierced her heart. Then she would be gayer than ever.

Much to Serena's surprise, Longford seem to be forsaking his rakehell ways to ensure Cecily's Season. He was so dutiful, attending both his sister and Serena, the matchmaking matrons began once again to urge their daughters to cast lures at the future duke, for obviously he'd mended his ways.

Halfway through the Season at Lady Jersey's ball, he bluntly informed both girls they were established firmly enough to satisfy even Their Graces, and promptly abandoned them to begin a scandalous interlude with a young married baroness whose elderly husband remained in the country. The tabbies were off! Both Cecily and Serena were continuously assailed by tidbits of gossip.

The next night Aunt Lavinia held her annual soiree to parade the lovelies for her son, or as some snidely remarked, "to parade her son for the lovelies." Frederick, stuffed into his coat, was immune to all but one.

"Cousin, dearest, do say you will assist my suit for the fair Lady Cecily. I've been captivated by her beauty since last winter at Avalon Hall," Frederick proposed to Serena after pulling her aside. "Did she receive the poem I penned to her eyelashes?"

His owl eyes, so like his mother's, blinked rapidly. His shirt points made it virtually impossible to turn his head and he moved with odd jerky contortions, looking at once like a crested jay.

Serena covered her smile at the mixed metaphors with her fan. "Frederick, the poem was lovely, but I've told you before Cecily regards you as a most charming friend," she repeated for what seemed like the hundredth time.

"I feared so." He languished. "Gossip has it Lady Cecily's heart has been given and she waits for someone's return." An expectant smile suffused his face, made ruddy by his too-constraining collar.

She wouldn't fall for that trap. "I wouldn't listen to idle gossip, Frederick, for it's usually inaccurate." Fanning herself briskly, for the soiree was a squeeze with virtually everyone in attendance, she attempted to fob off her cousin's inquiries. "I never pay heed to it myself."

"So like you, Serena, to be above such things. Mother says you're like your sainted papa. I don't care what anyone else says, you have my admiration for being so brave in the face of the unpleasant gossip about you and Longford."

Serena's moving fan clicked shut. Stunned, she stared back at Frederick, but he was already moving stiffly away. Gossip about Longford and her? The absurdity of it was such she instantly dismissed it from her mind.

That evening, much to her surprise, Longford waited up for their return. Since he stood propped against the library door, slowly swirling a snifter of brandy in his fingers, it was not too difficult to determine he'd been imbibing.

"What a pair of lovelies you are," he drawled, sipping at the brandy. "Cecily, Father has received three more offers for your hand and turned them down as you demanded he do at the beginning of this interminable Season. Their Graces are much too indulgent for your own good. Still determined to wait on Kendall, huh? You may end up on the shelf, brat!"

"How can you be so heartless, Long!" Cecily lifted her chin, sending him a pained look. "You know I have given my heart to Kendall. If you mean to be insulting, I'll have no part of it." Picking up the edge of her gown, she swept up the staircase without a backward glance.

"I want to talk to you alone anyway, Serena. Come into the library," he demanded before turning away to stroll lazily to the bottle and refill his glass.

She followed him for no other reason than to discover why he was being cruel to Cecily, whom he so obviously adored.

"It isn't like you to talk so to your sister."

He laughed once before flinging his head back and tossing the last of the brandy down his throat. "As you see, I'm not at my best tonight. Ever get bedeviled by ugly gossip, Serena?" he asked with a bluntness that sounded utterly sober, although he suddenly sat into a chair by the fireplace.

Holding herself stiffly erect, she looked calmly into his face and tried not to think about his resemblance to Blackwood. "I have no time for such nonsense. It's a waste of my energy."

His long mouth curved up at one end. "Well done, Serena. My mother's influence is clearly discernible." The hooded eyes slid over her slowly. "You've made a remarkable transformation from insipid country mouse to fascinating woman. Perhaps this time I really should take my cue from the gossiping tabbies and act accordingly."

He sprang up and lifted his hand to stroke her cheek with one finger.

She slapped it away. "Do stop being utterly absurd! I know exactly what you're up to." Exasperated past bearing, she glared at him. "Just inform me what this is all about. No doubt in time I'd find the proper way without your tortured guidance, but I haven't the patience for it now."

She had the privilege of seeing true surprise settle over his countenance.

"Obviously you've found it on your own. You've heard, I see. And dismissed the talk as the rubbish it is. I'm delighted your opinion of me isn't so low you'd believe I covet my brother's wife." He placed his glass on a side table and looked at it with distaste.

"Longford, unlike your sister, I know under all those layers of cynicism there really must be a heart. And I know it remains untouched by me, or anyone else."

Those hooded eyes studied her for a long moment. "Reverend Fitzwater's daughter, there are times when you amaze even me!" His genuine laughter echoed in the library even after he'd strolled out.

Immensely weary with all the currents swirling around her and the constant ache of Blackwood's absence kept tightly hidden inside, Serena wished for nothing but the forgetfulness of slumber. Before she could go up to her bedchamber, Cecily flew through the wide doorway to clasp her in a tight hug.

"I couldn't bear being at odds with Long, so came down to make amends and heard all!" she declared, releasing Serena to step back and smile so broadly, her dimple disappeared. "I'm delighted there isn't the slightest truth to what people are whispering."

Serena was utterly shocked to discover Cecily had heard the gossip and said nothing to her. "Why wouldn't you discuss this with me if you knew? Cecily, you weren't afraid it was true?"

"Long is quite dashing and handsome. Besides, he's a rake, and we women always lose our hearts to such men. It is something within us, believing we are the ones to save them from their fate," she returned calmly.

"But surely you would have hated me if I was unfaithful to Blackwood?" Serena's legs started to tremble and she sat in the chair Longford had just vacated.

"How could I hate you for loving both my brothers? It's easily done."

Her answer was so logical, Serena saw, at last, Cecily truly was her mother's daughter.

"But it's all right. Your undying affecting for Blackwood is stronger than Long's rakish appeal," Cecily finished with a dramatic sigh.

"In all honesty I must tell you rakes, your brother or any other, have never held any attraction for me. Perhaps in a novel it's so, but I believe most of us are drawn to other attributes. After all, Lord Kendall is not a rake, is he?"

"Lord Kendall is marvelous! So brave, so gallant, so handsome ... so..." Her eyes wide, Cecily obviously searched for more apt descriptions of her heart's desire. "...so absent," she finally concluded. "Serena, when will Kendall return? I don't know how much more I can bear."

Not being so poor-spirited to spoil Cecily's dramatic posture by reminding her she bore the loss of her husband, Serena patted the slumped shoulder. "We must be brave for just a while longer. These dreadful wars will end soon. And with that, Lord Kendall will return ... and Blackwood, also."

But Serena was proved wrong. For at the Season's end there was no happy news. She went to Avalon Landing after securing promises that any news would be sent straight through to her. The summer came and went. Fall promised a bountiful harvest, and the village was full of praise for the lady of the manor.

She returned to London, where the duke and duchess had stayed on so the Prince Regent's physician could attend His Grace, who continued failing.

It had been so long since word of Blackwood that when a letter finally arrived in October, both Cecily and the duchess demanded she read it aloud straightaway.

Dear Serena, we have finally arrived at Chesapeake Bay only to find chaos. The stores are inadequate, the accommodations worse. It's a low blow to the men after our difficult sea voyage. Sergeant Major Higgens is trying to rouse the men's lowered spirits while Jeffries assists Kendall and myself in procuring better equipment. Our orders are to march on their capital city, Washington it is called, and burn it if necessary. This does not sit well with the men or with me. Kendall sends his regards and as always I send my deep affection to all of you.

Blackwood

It was so vastly different from his other letters, which had been full of glory and valor, that they all stared at one another silently. Serena saw something flicker in the depths of the duchess's eyes. Perhaps she, too, had noticed the lack of personal affection or any whimsical reference to their chrysanthemum plant.

A few weeks later the duchess, pale-faced and without her usual grace, entered the conservatory, where Serena was fussing at the chrysanthemum, her thoughts, as always, centered on Blackwood.

"Serena, word has arrived from the War Office."

Something in the duchess's face brought her to her feet. Fear, greater than anything she had ever known, froze her into immobility.

Taking Serena's suddenly frozen hands, Her Grace squeezed them, bringing back life and warmth. "There has been a defeat at the bombardment of Fort McHenry. Matthew has been seriously injured and will be on the next boat home."

It took a few moments for the words to penetrate Serena's fear-numbed mind. She forced herself to speak calmly. "How serious are his injuries?"

Tears welled in Her Grace's eyes. "The dispatch didn't say. But he lives, Serena, and shall be returned to us."

"Yes." She nodded, unable to feel anything at this moment.

"Kendall and Jeffries will bring him safely home."

Now the tears did slide down Her Grace's pale cheeks. "Jeffries was killed trying to get Matthew to safety after he fell."

Without words, Serena went into her arms, each knowing what this loss must mean to Blackwood.

The news catapulted the entire household into action to prepare for Blackwood's arrival. Longford outfitted a carriage and drove to the coast. When the ship arrived he would immediately send a message with outriders so that all could be in readiness.

Before Blackwood was returned to her, another letter came. Obviously arriving on the same ship he had, it beat him to town. She opened it with trembling fingers and saw at once it was dated several weeks before.

> Serena, the bombardment of Fort McHenry began this morning and still continues with no end in sight. Sergeant Major Higgens fell today in a vain attempt to lead the men from utter defeat. His death serves no purpose, for word has been received we are negotiating peace, but we must fight on until it is settled. He could have been spared. My men's lives could have been spared, for this is all for naught. I know not what this night will bring. Tell my mother I now fully understand Shelly's words. "No man has a right to do an evil thing that good might come." Farewell. Blackwood

With terrifying certainty Serena realized this was not the letter of the man who, full of glory and confidence, left her on their wedding night.

Deceit was not a part of her nature, but she practiced it this night. Carefully folding the note several times, she locked it in the wooden box with the other often-read messages from Blackwood. The outriders had arrived and she could not share this note of despair with those who waited so hopefully.

With a fixed smile she drifted through the next day

determined to believe her fears were unfounded and that once she saw Blackwood, all would be as it had been during their brief, but glittering, courtship and marriage.

Cecily saw the carriage first from her post at the parlor window, where she'd been for hours worrying the golden tassels on the velvet drapes. "They are here!" she gasped, already moving toward the front door.

The duchess went after her, and Serena followed, her heart beating so hard against her ribs, it was difficult to breathe. Word had traveled quickly; the entire household suddenly appeared on the steps around them, except the duke, who was forced by illness to wait in his bedchamber.

Longford stepped out first, followed quickly by Kendall. Serena felt Cecily sob beside her as Kendall's bright green eyes surveyed her quickly before turning back to the open carriage door.

Pale fingers gripped the doorframe, and an instant later, Blackwood's face, still marked by an angry-looking wound across his forehead, appeared. Every giddy emotion Blackwood had ever inspired completely engulfed her, and without thought of anything but reaching him, she moved forward.

Helped by Kendall, he stepped down. Longford handed him a cane, and his mouth twisted in a grimace of pain as he walked toward them.

There was one moment of intense joy and reassurance when his eyes searched her out in the crowd moving forward to welcome him home. But her joy fled, replaced by cold, paralyzing fear, rooting her to a sudden halt, for the eyes looking at her were a stranger's.

With piercing clarity Longford's words came back to haunt her. "Someday he'll be forced to accept the world and us as we are … It is in your best interest to become the kind of woman up to that challenge."

Clearer than she'd ever known anything in her life, Serena knew that time had come.

Book Two

The Meeting

Home. Matt couldn't quite believe he was standing again on English soil. Perhaps the pain throbbing in his leg blurred his thoughts so the sea of people moving to greet him seemed unfocused. Nothing was quite real. Especially his wife.

His eyes sought out Serena—so beautiful and pure, so untouched by all the tragedy of the world. She moved toward him, then stopped abruptly. Could she see he had changed from the man she once knew? That he felt a stranger in his own home? Is that why she suddenly stared at him with such wide blue eyes?

Poppet reached him first, throwing her arms around him with her usual enthusiasm, but this time he couldn't sweep her up and twirl her around as was his habit.

"Oh, Matt, you're home at last!" she sobbed, her tears tickling his neck where she'd buried her face. "We've missed you so!"

With one arm he held her tight and tried not to grimace with the pain her weight added to the strain on his shattered leg. "Poppet, or should I call you Cecily, you're all grown-up."

"Well, of course! You've been away forever," she scolded with a hiccup before stepping away. "But you're home now and we shall never let you leave us again!"

His young sister had grown so dazzling, not even the tears streaking her cheeks detracted from her beauty. He saw admiration flair in Kendall's bright green eyes as she turned to him. Memory stirred something dormant in Matt's chest as, instead of curtsying, she extended her hand.

"Lord Kendall, welcome home."

"Lady Cecily, I echo Matt's sentiments. You are quite the lady now," Kendall laughed, pressing his lips to her fingers.

The stirring memory forced Matt's gaze back to Serena. Did she recall their first meeting when, instead of curtsying, she'd offered her hand and he'd taken it so eagerly?

That had happened to two different people—not the confident woman in a scoop-necked blue gown gathered high under her breasts by a velvet ribbon, no doubt in the height of fashion. And not the soldier, leaning heavily on his cane. Her keen eyes were lit with something he didn't recognize. It wasn't the sweet innocence he remembered.

But the changes were not hers alone. The scales had dropped from his eyes so he now saw himself and the world as they really were. Long had often called him an idealistic young fool; at last he understood what that meant.

Some things, however, were constant in a world spinning off its axis. His mother embraced him in rose-scented warmth: the security of childhood, of a world that would fall into place just as he wished. That he knew better now was a source of keen embarrassment. How could he have lived in his dream so long?

"Matthew." She released him. "It's wonderful to have you home. Your father awaits you upstairs. But first, I know there is someone you must be most eager to greet." With a last smile she stepped back and motioned Serena forward.

Of all his ideals, Serena had shone the brightest. Had he ever known her, really? Or had he only seen what he'd wanted to in her? Now he must learn to deal with the real woman, for she was in truth his wife.

The sunlight gleamed in her rich ebony curls threaded through by the same ribbon as her dress. The color exactly matched her eyes. He'd forgotten how thickly they were fringed with feathery black lashes which curled gently at the tips. He felt her hesitation; he saw it in the stiff set of her shoulders and the fixed smile not quite reaching those clear cornflower blue eyes. It was awkward, to meet thus, with all watching, after such a long separation.

She extended both hands. "Welcome home, my lord. You've been sorely missed."

He took one cool hand, still supporting his bad leg with the cane. When with a short glance she realized he couldn't take the other, she placed it over their clasped fingers. A gentle smile lit her face.

"You must be weary and hungry from your journey. The chef has spent days preparing all your favorite dishes. I know you remember how he holds us all hostage with his genius, so we mustn't keep him waiting."

This skillful handling of the strain between them surprised him. She'd been so quiet and unassuming when they wed. Or had she been? Perhaps he'd only seen her that way because he wished to.

Cecily laughed, sounding remarkably like their mother. "Serena's quite correct. Francois has outdone himself!"

"Yes, come. I know you all wish to freshen up before dinner. And perhaps, a visit for a few moments with His Grace." His mother placed her hand on Longford's arm, leading the way back into the house.

Matt followed slowly, with Serena beside him. He was oddly grateful she didn't try to assist him. In appreciation he slid her a smile which brought a light red flush to her slender neck and high cheekbones. She must feel the tension just as he did.

Cecily, holding Kendall's arm, brought up the rear. Matt caught snatches of her quiet questions about their journey and Kendall's brisk replies.

Serena remained silent, only nodding when he excused himself to make a long, painful climb to the second floor.

His short visit with his father left him cold with fear. The real evidence of the duke's declining health was not easy to accept. He couldn't bear the loss of anyone else he held dear to his heart. In the old days he could have hoped for a miracle, but his last battle had torn all prospect of hope from him.

Jeffries. The pain of loss thrust through him as clean and sure as the bayonet that had slashed his brow.

Long waited in his bedchamber.

"I shall find you a new valet tomorrow. But tonight I will have to do." Long spoke with none of his usual mockery as he poured water into the white bowl on the washstand.

"I don't need help. Nor do I wish a new valet."

Shrugging, Long stepped back to make way for him. It was slow going to lean on the cane with one hand and use the other to clean away the dust of travel, but he managed it, to his great relief.

Silence grew in the room. Silence and a feeling of estrangement. Where was the easy comradeship of the past? Matt turned from the small mirror. "I'm ready to go down now."

"So I see. And very well done. My compliments," Long drawled, flicking an invisible speck of lint from his impeccably tailored buff coat. "However, I shall still find you a valet as soon as possible."

"No! I want no one!" The sharpness of Matt's voice startled even him, cutting through the silence.

"Planning to spend the rest of your days polishing your own boots?" Long's mouth curled at the corner in a sneer. "Hardly a pastime for one of our nation's heroes."

"Cut line, Long! This is not a subject for your mockery. No one can ever replace Jeffries. He was more than just my batman, more than my friend. He was a part of my life for as long as I can remember. His loss is something I don't take lightly."

"And you think I do!" Matt's anger was well matched. "If you recall, we shared the same childhood. Jeffries sat me on my first horse; taught me most of what I know of good horseflesh. His loss is felt by all of us! No doubt once you stop wallowing in self-pity because you couldn't single-handedly wrest back the colonies without one drop of English blood being spilled, you'll see that for yourself."

If any other man spoke thus to him, Matt would have knocked him to the floor. Instead he stared into Long's flushed face. This show of emotion, when usually he affected languished boredom, cooled Matt's own anger.

"At the moment I'm not a worthy opponent, Long. Don't bother to take up your weapons against me. This is neither the time nor the place to discuss each other's shortcomings. Of which we both have ample."

With a nod, Long strolled toward the door and opened it

for Matt to pass through.

"As your older brother, I claim the right to say one last thing before we join the others." Long's voice dropped to an even tone. They stood face-to-face within the wide, rectangular doorway. Of a height, they stared evenly into each other's eyes.

"Matt, the world, the people who care about you, haven't changed. Everything is the same as it's always been. Only you have changed."

With that direct thrust, Long strolled almost casually out of the room and down the stairs, leaving Matt staring after him.

Matt knew he was correct. During the hospital fever that wracked his body after his injuries had been treated, despite the raw ache of loss, Matt had realized he had to go on. He had survived! Now it was up to him to chart a new course for his life, to find new meaning. Sometimes he wondered why he had been spared; others hadn't. Jeffries, rattling in death, his body protectively shielding Matt from the enemy. Higgens, rising up from the ground, rallying the men with his battle cry. And the men themselves moaning in death all around him. And for what? For what good and noble purpose was this evil done? For nothing.

Meaningless. As his own life had become in that instant. Suddenly he realized it wasn't just himself. He had a wife, Serena. He had to face her. She had innocently wed one man and now would be forced to accept another.

The high-ceilinged dining room had been set as for a party. Six shining candelabras blazed with light, illuminating the fine porcelain and twinkling crystal. The duchess presided at one end, Matt at her side. Serena sat next to him, across from Kendall. A footman stood behind each chair, eager to present Francois's creations.

Kendall, loud in his appreciation of such culinary delights, kept up a steady stream of conversation concerning the quality of dining in America and aboard ship during their long voyage home.

Across from him, Cecily was all rapt attention, her eyes feasting on his face instead of the delicacies so painstakingly prepared.

Serena was no better, only toying with her food while pretending to pay attention to the conversation between Her Grace, Kendall, and Longford. In truth her thoughts were centered on only one thing—the man sitting so quietly beside her. Blackwood was neither the fairy-tale hero she'd wed so quickly nor the man she'd envisioned in the months living with his family and his belongings, learning what books and music he loved, learning what his life had been like before they met.

He was still startlingly handsome, perhaps even more so now the square chin was firmer, and the face chiseled down. Not even the wound across his wide brow, or his forced, stiff gait where once he'd moved with such confidence, distracted from his appeal in her eyes. Yet in all her dreams of his return, never had she imagined this aloof chasm between them, not even after his letters changed. Her husband was a stranger to her.

Her nerves were so taut, she nearly jumped when the duchess rose, announcing they would leave the men to their port.

With a white line of pain around his tight lips, Blackwood pushed himself to his feet.

"If you'll all excuse me, I'll retire early myself." He shot a hard look at Longford, who responded by continuing to twirl his wineglass between his fingers. "Tomorrow I look forward to hearing all the news while I've been away."

Finally he turned to her with just the merest shadow of his old whimsical smile. A small ache of joy tightened her throat. Somewhere hidden behind the cool, detached exterior he presented, somewhere deep inside, was the man she had married.

As he made his way slowly from the room, the thought came to her again that while he was away he'd had no opportunity to learn more about her, so still clung to the images of their brief marriage. Now he'd returned, could he find the reality wanting? Joy turned to pain, making it hard to keep her tears locked behind dry eyes.

Gratefully she followed Her Grace and Cecily into the small parlor. A maid placed a tea tray before the couch where the duchess gracefully reclined.

"Lord Kendall is just as I remembered him," Cecily sighed, posing prettily in a chair beside her mother.

"Yes. However, your brother is not." The hard note in the duchess's usually musical voice caused Cecily unconsciously to sit up straighter and Serena to stand rooted to the floor, twisting her trembling fingers together before her.

"He has been hurtfully disillusioned," the duchess continued with the same firmness.

Serena leaned forward, tensely awaiting Her Grace's assessment. If anyone could show her the way to help him, it would be his mother.

"I pride myself on my sons' fine minds and keen insights. Just as someday Richard's cynicism will be tempered, Matt's idealism has been shattered in ways which will be difficult for him to pick up the pieces and form a new pattern. We must be patient and assist him in any way we can."

"But how can we best help him, Mother?" Cecily asked eagerly. "I want the old Matt back, prosy as ever."

"That we shall never have, Cecily, nor should we wish it for Matthew's sake." Gracefully lifting the teapot, she poured the dark liquid into white cups. "As to how we can best help him, we must each find our own way."

The exasperated look Cecily flashed Serena spoke volumes. Her Grace obviously expected them to take appropriate action, but would offer no specific suggestions.

"I believe I shall forgo tea and retire to my bedchamber." Frustrated, Serena wanted time to consider a plan of attack. Blackwood was her husband—there must be some way to reach him.

She found none as she paced back and forth across the delicate blue and cream carpet. Serena stared at the dark wooden door separating her bedchamber from his. Should she knock on the door and ask if he needed any assistance?

Instinct told her Blackwood would not accept that.

Glancing at the ticking clock on the mantel, she realized she'd already wasted twenty minutes uselessly fretting about her further actions. Should she go on as if he weren't there?

That seemed untenable to her.

She stopped in front of the door. Should she be so bold as to just assume he would wish to spend his first night at home with his wife after such a lengthy absence? Should she demand he do so?

The naive, innocent child Blackwood had married would never be so bold, but Serena was a woman now, all due to him. He had awakened her to the wonder of romance. He had provided all the opportunities for her to learn and grow, to take responsibility for an entire estate. She had followed her instincts and she had done well in every other endeavor. Why did she feel so helpless now?

Vainly she sought for an insight into the best way to approach her husband. A loud crash on the other side of the door startled her into action. Without a moment's hesitation, she pushed the door wide and entered his chamber.

Instantly he turned a pale, pain-tightened face toward her. Blackwood must have stumbled before he fell into the chair and toppled over the table beside it. His cane lay too far away for him to reach it.

Without words, she placed the small rosewood table back in position and leaned his cane against the chair. Only then did she meet his dark, anguished eyes.

"I'm sorry I disturbed you. I'm often clumsy these days." He shrugged, his glance flicking toward his cane. "Perhaps I should move to another chamber so—"

"Of course not. These are your ... our rooms," she interrupted without thinking, and then regretted it as his gaze studied her face.

"Serena, very soon we must talk about all that has transpired while I've been away."

"We could do so tonight if you wish." She hoped her words didn't sound as unseemingly eager to his ears as they did to hers.

He pushed himself to his feet. "No, I'm afraid tonight is not the time. Tomorrow perhaps. Rest well, Serena, and I shall try not to disturb you again."

His dismissal left her no other choice but to leave him.

Not so subtly, she allowed the door to remain open between the rooms. Trying for a semblance of normalcy, she began to take down her hair, placing the pins in a tortoiseshell box on her dressing table.

There was a prolonged silence while she brushed through her hair. Finally the door shut behind her.

She crossed the room to lean weakly against it, closing her eyes to take deep, even breaths, trying to still the pulse pounding through her. Where was the confident, glorious man who'd swept her off her feet? He'd been so sure she was the woman he'd sought. There had been nothing tentative in any of his actions toward her before. Now hesitation pervaded every word and action between them.

Confusion coiled fingers through every fiber of her being, making it difficult to think, to do anything but feel. And she was uncertain now of even that. What should she be feeling?

The maid already had water poured into the bowl on the washstand and her white cotton gown laid across the foot of the bed. As rapidly as she could, she was between the cool, crisp sheets, burying her cheek in the pillow, desiring the solace of slumber. Unable to find just the right position to bring peace to her weary body, she tossed and turned until the covers were a tumbled heap around her.

Staring wide-eyed at the underside of the canopy above her, she heard the tall clock in the hallway chime the hour. It was already the morrow, and still she couldn't find the forgetfulness of sleep she so desperately sought.

A cry ripped through the stillness. She sat bolt upright, staring toward the door, barely discernible in the shadowing glow of the dying fire.

Yes, there it was again! There could be no doubt the sound came from Blackwood's chamber. Barefoot, she crept across the room to rest her ear against the wood.

Now she could discern snatches of sentences, but from this distance, couldn't understand the meaning. A loud, quick burst of words followed by a low moan tore at her heart.

Whether this was the right way or no, she couldn't just

stand here and listen to Blackwood suffer. Quietly she pushed the door open and entered his chamber once again.

He sprawled across the bed, the dying embers casting a glow which gleamed off his broad, bare chest. The sheet was tangled low around his hips, revealing he wore nothing.

Something hot and tight coiled low in her stomach. She pushed it away to slip onto the side of the bed and softly touch his shoulder.

"Matthew, wake up, it's only a bad dream."

Her quiet words brought no relief as, eyes closed, his head twisted back and forth on the pillow.

"The right flank! Must protect the men! Higgens! Oh, no!" he moaned through dry lips.

"Matt," she said louder, gripping his shoulder more tightly with her fingers, desperate now to end his suffering.

Still the nightmare held him. "Must protect the right flank! No, Jeffries! Leave me! Leave me before it's too late!" he cried with such anguish tears sprang to her eyes.

Leaning her weight against his chest to capture both moving shoulders in her hands, her hair fell forward around his face as she spoke directly to him. "Matt, you must wake up! Matt, wake up!"

He opened his eyes within the curtain of her hair. An instant later, total awareness widened his eyes and she forced herself to move back from him to tangle her trembling fingers within the folds of her night shift.

"Was it the dreams?" he asked harshly, drawing the sheet up over his chest.

"Nightmares more like," she whispered in return, her heart pounding painfully against her ribs.

He nodded, pushing himself higher against the headboard to look squarely into her eyes. The shadows made him look as young as he'd appeared when they met. "It seems I've disturbed you yet again."

"You didn't disturb me. I want to help you. After all, I'm your wife," she reminded him.

"This isn't something I can discuss with you. With anyone."

His dark eyes were as mesmerizing as ever as they bore into her as if seeking her soul. "Serena, it must be apparent to you I'm not the man you wed. That idealistic young fool is gone forever." He rubbed absently at his injured leg. "The man who remains would never be so foolish as that arrogant youngster."

"We've all changed during our separation. I, too, am no longer as I was when we met." Was it right? Would it make things better to point out she'd also changed, even though she'd promised she wouldn't?

"Yes, I can see it." He nodded. "You no longer chew on your lower lip."

That he remembered such an insignificant thing made her smile. "You remember that? Then perhaps you also remember our few hours of happiness as husband and wife."

She could see by the sudden stiffening of his shoulders she'd shocked him by alluding to their hours of intimacy.

"I can see you still possess your blunt honesty," he said evenly, once again rubbing at his thigh. "I'll be honest in return. Perhaps, after all, it's best to confront everything now to prevent any further pain I might cause you."

If she'd once thought his eyes dark pools in which to drown, they were even more so now; and drowning she was with no hope of safety in sight.

"Serena, I regret we're strangers now. Whatever drew you to me no longer exists. I'm sorry for it because it's unfair to saddle you with this union. In time I'm sure we can come to some understanding which will suit us both."

These cynical words, where once he'd spoken with such romantic lyric, closed in like deep, dark water over her head.

"You regret our marriage because you find me different from the naïve child I once was?" Vainly she sought to break the surface.

"I regret that young girl so innocently gave her heart to someone who no longer exists," he answered gently. "As you say, you are no longer that young girl, nor am I that boy."

Pain caused her to gasp in confusion. The intake of air seemed to restore her ability to move. She leapt to her feet, barely containing her anger. "Then we shall have to discover if who we have become can find any common threads to weave a new beginning."

Pride spun her on her bare feet and kept her back ramrod straight until she made it into her own bedchamber. This time she did close the door behind her. Only then did she give in to the ache tearing her insides to bits and let her shoulders slump forward as tears streamed down her face.

In truth he was no longer the fairy-tale hero of her first flush of romance. Nor was he the man she'd begun to know and love through his letters and the things he'd once cared about.

What was left?

The Courtship

Dawn had given way to dazzling winter sunshine by the time Serena awoke. Copious tears had finally succumbed to the oblivion of slumber. She stretched languorously, then remembered—Blackwood was home. Obviously someone had stopped her maid from waking her with her usual breakfast. Perhaps the duchess had done so in the anticipation Serena might not be alone in her bed.

Memory of the confrontation in the intimacy of her husband's chamber brought the same anger-laced pain: anger at herself, at Blackwood, at the war, at all that separated them; and pain for the happiness lost. It wasn't fair! She knew what she wanted, but it seemed impossible—she yearned to go back to those feelings he had inspired in her so long ago. She wanted her husband, heart-whole, charming, and full of ideals, returned to her.

She freely admitted she was no longer as naive and blindly romantic as she'd once been. And with aching regret she acknowledged Blackwood's view of life was not as glitteringly noble and pure as it had been. But surely there must be something left, some in-between stage where they could come together and recapture all they had lost.

She stared at the closed door that separated them and willed it to open. Suddenly she wanted her father, like a child trusting that a parent could make everything right again. Perhaps if she went back to the beginning, if she recaptured what had been, she could find something to reinspire Blackwood's regard.

Slipping on her robe, she went to the small cherrywood desk and penned a letter inviting both her father and Buckle to spend the holiday in London. When the letter was waxed and sealed, she rang for her maid. There was no use in putting it off a moment more; she must simply face whatever painful disclosures this day might bring.

Descending the staircase, she held her head high, bolstered by a new frock of jonquil satin with a deep flounce at the hemline and long, tight sleeves ending in a small ruffle over her hands. Chin up, she marched into the dining room and was promptly deflated to find her brave front was to no avail. The only person to witness it was a footman standing at rigid attention by the sideboard laden with silver-covered dishes.

"I had no idea I was so late," Serena muttered, slipping onto the chair he held for her. "Has everyone else already been served luncheon?"

"The Marquess of Longford and Lord Kendall left this morning for their clubs. Her Grace and Lady Cecily dined early as they had appointments on Bond Street."

"And Lord Blackwood?" she prompted with what she hoped was a show of calm interest.

"A tray in his room, my lady." With a deferential nod he turned to prepare her a plate of chops smothered in a mushroom sauce, with a side of buttered peas, followed by a fruit trifle with custard.

Under his eagle eye she felt compelled to do more than move the food about on her plate. As soon as she was able, she escaped to the conservatory. It had become a favorite retreat. Frost pictures decorated the windows, letting light through to pattern the stone floor. She sat in one small pool of sunshine to tend the chrysanthemum plant. It was at the end of its blooming season. She pinched off the dead flowers but left four faded blooms that were not completely gone.

She was concentrating so on the plant, the awareness of being watched came unexpectedly. Swiveling around, she found Blackwood, near the fountain, staring at her.

If he hadn't been leaning on his cane, he would have looked perfectly normal, his long legs encased in tan unmentionables, his navy jacket fitting a bit loosely over a plain white shirt. Patterns of light dappled him with sunshine as he moved slowly toward her, the cane tapping an uneven rhythm upon the stone floor.

"Good afternoon, Serena." His smile didn't quite reach his rich, dark eyes. "What are you tending so diligently?"

"Our chrysanthemum plant. It's thriving just as you requested it should." Instinct led her to be quietly frank. "Do you recall sending it here to me before boarding ship for the Peninsula?"

A red flush crept up the strong bones of his face. "A romantic fancy." He shrugged. "I'm sorry it caused you such inconvenience. You should have turned it over to the gardener to tend."

"Certainly not! Horticulture is a great interest of mine. I'm quite good at it."

Perhaps it was surprise at her vehemence that lifted his brows. "So I see. I had no idea you were such an expert gardener."

"How could you? We knew very little of one another's interests when we wed." Was it the anger making her so blunt? Or was it some other force within her?

"You're right, of course." His long mouth curled in a wry smile. "I must apologize, I suppose, for being so impetuous. If we had been wiser, perhaps—"

"Wisdom had naught to do with it," she interrupted, a fine edge of anger bringing her to her feet. Why must he continually allude to their marriage as if it were a mistake? Naught could be done now. Surely they could deal together better than this. "I was as impetuous as you. The … attraction I felt for you was every bit as strong as what you believed you felt for me." Serena could feel a hot flush rise up from her chest to burn her cheeks. How could he fail to hear her heart pounding as he stared at her silently? He took a tentative step forward.

"Oh, here you both are!" exclaimed Cecily, shattering the tense moment so abruptly, Serena sat back down upon the bench, for her knees were trembling.

After pressing a quick kiss upon Blackwood's cheek, Cecily danced over to sit beside Serena and squeezed her hand.

"While shopping on Bond Street, Mother and I met the Duchess of Southerland. She told us several of our friends are staying in town for the holidays. So we've come up with the most wonderful plan! A ball to welcome in the New Year and celebrate Matt's return to us. Is that not marvelous?"

"Marvelous."

They replied in unison, one voice amazed, the other sarcastic.

As she sprang up, Cecily's dimple came and went in her pink cheek. "Come along, Serena; let us make our guest list. Mother says we must start our plans immediately as the holidays are nearly upon us."

Blowing her brother a kiss, Cecily gripped Serena's hand and nearly pulled her from the conservatory, leaving Blackwood staring after them, a quizzical curve to his mouth.

"Cecily, what are you up to?" Serena demanded, stumbling after her determined sister-in-law.

"Well, Mother says we must find our own path to help Matt regain his aplomb. Mine is to plunge him immediately back into the social whirl." Stopping in the hallway, Cecily let go of Serena's hand to look at her with wide, dark eyes. "Remember, it was at a ball that he swept you off your feet. Perhaps at this one you can do likewise. I certainly plan to do so to Lord Kendall!"

Cecily's confidence bolstered Serena through the next few weeks as the holidays descended upon them and nothing changed in Blackwood's cool detachment. At night she could sometimes hear him in the grips of one of his nightmares, but she forced herself to bury her face in the pillows and ignore the overpowering urge to offer comfort. He'd said he couldn't discuss it with her.

Until he could bring himself to confide in her the terrors of those dreams, her presence would only add weight to his already heavy burden.

Blackwood appeared to be most at ease with Longford and Kendall when they spent evenings in the library over port and cards. His afternoons were dedicated to reading the newest political treatises to the duke and discussing the ramifications to the country of the long and expensive French wars. In his dealings with his father, Blackwood displayed a gentleness and intelligence that brought a little catch to her throat whenever she saw them together.

To her he was unfailingly polite and courteous, but the door between them was as firmly shut as the one in their chambers.

By the time her father and Buckle arrived on Christmas Eve, Serena's nerves were ready to shatter from the strain of pretending to view all and sundry with the same cool detachment Blackwood displayed.

She could feel Buckle's blue eyes searching her face throughout the Christmas festivities. On the night of the ball Buckle appeared at her bedchamber and dismissed the maid, stating in no uncertain terms that she would do what was necessary for Serena's toilette.

Matter-of-factly Buckle fastened the catches at the back of the silvery silk gown Serena had chosen to wear because it reminded her so forcibly of one she'd worn in her first Season; except this gown was cut deep over her breasts, held up only by small sleeves poised low on her shoulders.

"Dear child, you look breathtaking. Even though these London fashions are a mite shocking to we country folk," Buckle chuckled good-naturedly.

Smiling, Serena studied herself in the mirror as Buckle expertly brushed her hair high on her head and let one curl fall along her throat.

"There! You shall dazzle your husband tonight."

In the mirror, their eyes met and held. There could be no pretense with Buckle. "I'm afraid our reunion hasn't been all I'd hoped," Serena said softly.

"I know, dear child. I've been watching the two of you and growing more concerned every moment." The rosebud mouth straightened in sorrow. "Can you tell me why?"

"He's changed so, Buckle."

"So have you," she replied.

"Yes, we're no longer the same impetuous children who wed so quickly. I wish there was some way to go back to that time."

"Would you really wish it? What did you truly know of Lord Blackwood then?"

As she continued to hold Buckle's gaze in the mirror, heat

flared in Serena's face. "Nothing but how he made me feel."

"And what have you learned about him since then?" Buckle asked with great gentleness.

Serena blinked rapidly to force her eyes to hold their tears. "He is gentle and intelligent. Obviously brave. But he has acquired an adamant detachment which pushes me away."

"Although he's no longer your romantic hero, it seems to me there is much in him to admire. Perhaps instead of wishing for what was, you might consider what could be."

Clasping the gnarled hand that still fussed with her curl, Serena pressed it to her lips before turning to face Buckle. "You are as wise as Father."

The apple cheeks glowed scarlet as pale blue eyes widened in unfeigned shock. "Dear child, your father is a great scholar. 'Tis just simple country logic I possess."

"You've given me much to ponder."

"Ponder nothing this night but enjoyment," Buckle demanded, urging her into the hallway. "I'll be watching with the other servants in the minstrel gallery, so enjoy yourself or I'll give you a scolding."

Serena's smile lingered as she descended the stairs. She couldn't remember the last time Buckle had scolded her. To give her former nursemaid no cause for concern, Serena swept into the ball, head held high, displaying more confidence than she truly possessed.

The duchess, in black silk with diamonds sparkling at her throat and ears, greeted her guests at the doorway. The duke was seated in a small alcove off the main ballroom, already surrounded by distinguished cronies. Serena caught a glimpse of both Longford and Blackwood among them.

Cecily, as always, was surrounded by admirers, including cousin Frederick, who was affecting a particularly ambitious cravat which fell quite short of perfection.

It was particularly gratifying to be surrounded by a number of admirers herself since her husband appeared indifferent. If she focused on being amusing, she could stop thinking about him entirely. Often she glanced toward the minstrel gallery, but couldn't find Buckle's round, sweet face among the servants watching from above.

Lowering her eyes, she was startled to find Longford advancing upon her.

"Her Grace has decreed I should lead you out for the first waltz since Matt is unable to dance."

Her gaze slid over his shoulder, searching the room.

"He's with Father," Longford added, before placing her hand on his arm, whisking her away from her court of admirers and onto the dance floor.

As they twirled around the room amidst the other dancers, Serena relaxed, for Longford was well versed in the steps. Since he wasn't bothering to make polite conversation, she was able to continue her perusal of the gallery. At last she saw dear Buckle waving at her. Lifting her hand from Longford's shoulder, she blew her a kiss.

His gaze instantly followed. "Who are you blowing kisses to?" he inquired lazily.

"Buckle. She's watching with the other servants."

Meeting her eyes, he gave her a lopsided smile. "There is still a bit of the reverend's daughter in our polished London beauty, isn't there? Just as there remains a streak of idealism in Matt, although he denies all he once held dear. Do you recall I once warned you this would come to pass one day?"

"Yes, I believe you thought me unworthy of the task now at hand," she responded quietly.

"And are you?" he asked harshly, his hooded eyelids nearly shut. "Can you help Matt rediscover himself?"

Pride lifted her chin. "There are many avenues to the same place. I am searching for the right one."

"By God, my mother has truly taught you well! I shall cease worrying. Between Her Grace, my incorrigible sister, and you, Matt hasn't a prayer of anything short of a full recovery to his former heroic self."

Never quite certain where Longford's real intentions lay—was he sincere or was this a bit of mockery from his restless intellect?—she felt it necessary to put him in his place. "If that is the case, then you should beware your own armor of cynicism lest we decide to take *you* in hand."

Forgetting the waltz in progress and the august assembly, Long gave way to rich laughter, which drew several eyes to where they glided across the floor.

Over Longford's shoulder she saw the laughter had drawn Blackwood's attention also. He was studying them with unfathomable eyes. If only she could read what the depths held. If only she could be sure the path she'd chosen was correct.

Long spun Serena out of Matt's view.

"Your brother certainly enjoys himself with your wife. Remember the night you first clapped eyes on her?" Kendall laughed between sips of champagne.

Matt had been studying her glowing skin in the candlelight and the way the long ebony curl fell down her throat to lie above the curve of her breasts, and he could find nothing of the simple, sweet girl who'd first drawn his eyes. How pompous he must have appeared in those days, assuming everyone and everything fit into his scheme of things! Whatever had possessed Serena to go along with his ridiculous romantic notion? She said she was as impetuous as he. But he found that hard to believe as he watched the confident and clearheaded way she conducted herself now.

"She's certainly changed a great deal since then," he finally answered carefully.

"She was a pretty little thing then. Now she's a beautiful woman. Thought you'd run mad that night, remember?"

This time Kendall's laughter caused Matt to flick his friend a cool look. He found Kendall's eyes had wandered from Serena to Cecily, who was in high gig surrounded by several devoted beaus.

"Now I see running mad might hold a certain appeal," Kendall continued somewhat fiercely. Draining his champagne glass, he placed it on the tray of a passing footman before sliding Matt a sheepish grin. "I'm off to rescue your sister."

A moment later he had displaced her circle, completely monopolizing her.

Once, Matt had viewed this glittering scene with eyes that chose to see only the glamour and the camaraderie. Life had been full of goodness. Now he watched and speculated, seeking deeper motivations. But viewing his world with these new eyes didn't make him any happier.

Rubbing absently at his thigh, he studied Long and Serena for another minute, trying to forget the odd twist in his gut. Shrugging it off, he made his way across the ballroom, apologized to his mother for his uncharacteristic tiredness, and retired.

A few weeks later, when Long informed him he would be staying in London with their parents instead of taking the much-anticipated trip to Avalon Landing with Matt, and then Serena immediately suggested that perhaps they, too, should postpone their trip to Sussex, the odd little twist returned. His gut tightened with the unbidden thought that Long was a notorious womanizer. Surely he hadn't turned his practiced eye upon his brother's wife? And she in turn responded? Once, he would never have thought of such a possibility. Now he was sickened that he had. Turning away in disgust—how low could he sink, to suspect his own flesh and blood—he curtly informed her he was leaving for the Landing in a fortnight, and whoever wished to accompany him was welcome.

On a crisp February morning with the sun's brilliance reflecting off a light layer of new snow, Kendall tucked Cecily and Serena into a large traveling carriage and mounted his horse. Matt was doubly glad his leg had improved sufficiently to ride, and he could skip the embarrassing confinement of the coach. For the tension between himself and his wife had increased tenfold. Having been married so briefly and now coming together virtual strangers was not Serena's fault. It was his. So it was his duty to set it straight. Why couldn't he just move ahead with his life and be satisfied with the kind of union many members of the *ton* endured? A marriage of convenience, where the parties came together when necessary but otherwise lived their own lives, was common enough. Apparently there still lurked, although nearly vanquished, a thread of romantic idealism in him, a vision of what he wished the world to be. He just no longer had the strength to make it happen.

In London he had discovered his wife had grown from the inexperienced and easily impressed ingenue to a polished woman of the *ton*, able to take her place in every social situation. In the country he was astonished at her astute management. She had wrought unbelievable changes at the Landing.

The house always had a comfortable, slightly shabby bachelor feel about it. Her redecoration was bang up to the minute yet still set a comfortable, homey feel, even in the public rooms. Although the style was charming, nothing was as he remembered. He tried to be as noncommittal as possible, but he saw in Serena's strained countenance that she recognized his feelings.

He was glad she wasn't present when he conducted his interview with Mr. Stockton.

"Lady Blackwood did what?" he demanded, unable to keep utter disbelief out of his voice.

"Well, my lord, besides ordering new fences and a refurbishing of all the cottages, she fixed it up with the parson's wife to have a teacher come in to learn the village children their letters."

Not even his avant-garde mother had ever been so bold. Matt remembered Long's letter that Serena had taken the Landing in hand. It had been full of admiration. But it had not specified how far she had gone. Matt had been concerned the decorating might be too taxing for his fragile wife. Obviously he'd been as wrong about her as everything else.

"What else?" he asked quietly.

"Well, my lord, after the young Watleys was killed on the Peninsula, the widow Watley had to give up her cottage to a new tenant. The land, you know. I couldn't just let it lie. Lady Blackwood moved her into that wee cottage just above the stream that's always vacant on account it has no land to speak of. She ordered Stevens to send her all the mending from the house and ordered me to pay her a wage for her work. Told me she was sure you'd want to take care of the widow since her family has always served the estate so well."

A hot flush of embarrassment rose from his chest. "I see." Flipping through the account book, Matt considered his next question. "I believe my brother, the Marquess of Longford, was in residence when all these changes were requested. Did he have nothing to say?"

"My lord, I did appeal to the marquess for guidance. He informed me I should honor her ladyship's requests as I would your own."

What could Long have been thinking of? Although nothing seemed amiss, before he said another word, Matt had to see for himself.

"I shall ride out myself and inspect the changes, Stockton. That will be all."

The country air was crisp and clean; for the first time in months he felt truly alive again. He gave his horse its head. The wintery sea wind ruffled his hair and chilled his face; he saw everything around him with sharper, clearer eyes.

His first stop was the Browns' newly whitewashed cottage with fresh thatch on the roof. He was greeted warmly and urged into the snug kitchen to share a cup of hot cider. He'd never seen Mrs. Brown when she wasn't increasing, and once again she was with child. Matt counted eight children at the fire; the oldest girl could be no more than ten.

"My yield is up from last year, my lord," Daniel Brown informed him with his grizzled head held high. "The young ones been more of a help last season. Must thank your lordship for that. Now the roof don't leak, they sleep all snug and dry in the loft, so I'm ready for a hard day's work."

"I see the repairs were of benefit then," Blackwood remarked, sipping at the heavy brown earthenware mug.

"Aye. And me Polly here learned her letters." Pride lightened his weathered face. "Reads to the wee ones so Mrs. Brown can rest awhile. Right content we are, my lord, thanks be to your good graces."

Matt was compelled to insure thanks be given where it was deserved. "It's her ladyship's good graces you must thank. I'm afraid I've been absent so long, I wasn't aware of your needs."

"Aye, protecting us from Boney." Daniel Brown nodded with real enthusiasm. "Right proud to be tenants of one of our nation's heroes. Right proud to have the good graces of a great lady like yours."

Brown's sentiments were echoed at each of the cottages where Matt called. Even Reverend Morton was filled with praise for his wife and congratulated his lordship on a most excellent choice.

His last stop was the small cottage on the high bank along a narrow, meandering stream, now a ribbon of ice. He recognized linen from the Landing neatly folded in a basket near the door. Mrs. Watley's strong tea warmed and relaxed him, so he spread out his legs before the small fireplace. He remembered her sons; although a few years younger, they had often raced their mounts through the village.

He spoke of battle and the bravery of the soldiers. Platitudes only, which he no longer believed, but which brought a fierce light of pride to her face.

"The footman what's brought me yonder linens told me your lordship was in residence again." Bustling up from her chair, Mrs. Watley carefully lifted a tissue-wrapped package from the table and held it out to him. "Been workin' on this here gift for her ladyship."

Nodding, he took it from her fingers. "I'll see my wife receives it. Are you content here, Mrs. Watley?"

Her lined, round face broke into a smile. "Miss not havin' anyone to look after. But grateful I am to have such a snug place. Your lordship be a hero and a generous man."

His lordship was confused and more than a little chagrined that while he was lamenting the world was not truly the glorious place he'd believed, Serena had set about trying to make it more so.

Riding slowly back to the Landing, he had plenty of time to consider the changes she'd wrought. The realization that Serena was not a fragile ideal to be cherished and protected, but a woman, and even more than he'd ever dreamed, a woman to share and grow with, stirred new feelings which gave him even more to think about.

When they finally met at supper, he could only stare with curiosity at the woman he'd wed, but surely never really known.

"Looked for you to go riding, Matt. Then found you'd gone off without me," Kendall scolded, although his eyes were as merry as ever. "Your sister consented to entertaining me with a hand of whist, so you're excused for your desertion."

Cecily sent Kendall a dimpled smile of such sweetness, Matt was thunderstruck. His sister had without a doubt set her sights on Kendall. The infatuation wasn't new to Matt, but her obvious intent was staggering. Was his friend aware? Before he could gauge Kendall's reaction, Cecily turned her dark eyes upon him.

"Matt, what do you think of the wondrous changes Serena has made? Is she not truly amazing?" Cecily gushed, much to Serena's obvious embarrassment.

Serena shot his sister a look he couldn't decipher, but which caused Cecily to toy nervously with her lamb stew.

"I'm sure your brother will have his own opinions of the changes I've made at the Landing," she said quietly, lifting her chin to send him a smile that was strained.

"Yes, I have my own opinion." Leaning back, he twirled his wineglass between his fingers. "I'm in complete agreement with Cecily."

"You are!" Cecily gasped in surprise, but quickly recovered to flash Serena a triumphant look.

Serena sat silently staring at him in bewilderment.

"In that case, perhaps you'll be favorable to a few of my ideas, brother dear."

Kendall gazed at her indulgently. Matt was startled. Had his own infatuation been so blatant? Did all men make fools of themselves thus?

"Lord Kendall says he's never had the pleasure of viewing a Roman ruin. While the fair weather lasts, I thought we could ride out, stopping at the White Feathers for lunch."

Shrugging, Matt nodded his agreement, taking a quick peek at Serena, who stared back at him agog. He had been more obvious than he'd thought in his first uneasiness about all the changes here. His change of heart seemed to stun her.

"It sounds a pleasant diversion. Perhaps we should also plan a country ball. It's been years since I've seen some of our neighbors. Would that be too much trouble, Serena?"

Her cornflower blue eyes widened in surprise, but her cherry lips curled in a tentative smile. "Of course not, my lord. Cecily and I shall plan it immediately."

Their eyes locked and for just an instant something stirred low in his gut. Not the odd twist the sight of Serena and Long dancing had caused, but something different and stronger. Perhaps there was hope for them yet.

Round and round his mind whirled in debate. It was actually a relief to escape to his room at last, although usually he didn't look forward to the night and the dreams that continued to haunt him. As he undressed he remembered the package he'd been given that afternoon and the promise he'd made to deliver it quickly.

He pulled on a dressing gown, but stopped at the door between their rooms. It had remained firmly closed since that one night he'd rejected her help. What would she think if he knocked?

It was only the promise that urged him on. Besides, he reasoned, her maid would answer. Coward, he chided himself, and knocked.

The door swung open. Serena, her ebony curls cascading over her shoulders, stood before him clad only in a long-sleeved nightshift of finely tucked lawn.

"Blackwood, are you all right?" she asked hoarsely, her gaze scanning him carefully.

"Yes." Raising his eyebrows in surprise at her anxious tone, he shrugged uneasily. "I merely forgot to give you a gift Mrs. Watley entrusted me to present."

Scarlet flooded her pale cheeks. "I was concerned because you've never before ... Never mind!" Shaking her head, she put her hand out for the package, revealing how transparent the gown actually was. "Thank you for bringing me the gift. How is Mrs. Watley?" she asked as she carefully unwrapped the package.

"Content. Thanks to your kindness." Propped against the doorframe, he watched curiously. "What is it?"

She lifted a tiny garment from the cocoon of tissue. They both realized what it was at the same instant—an infant gown with beautiful embroidery at the hem and along the tiny ruffled neckline.

Her eyes, blue pools of confusion, lifted to his, stirring to life an ache in his chest. His heart gave one single stroke.

"It's beautiful. She does fine work." He forced his tones to be even despite the blood pounding loudly through his veins.

She nodded, folding the tiny garment back into its wrappings. "I must ride out and thank her." Lifting her chin, she gave him a fleeting smile. "Rest well, my lord."

Nodding, he slowly closed the door and leaned his forehead against it. Breathing deeply, he tried to still his pulse. This whole day had provided him with a new perspective. Perhaps that was why he could now see the thread with which he could weave something of meaning with his life.

Serena leaned her hot forehead against the door, Mrs. Watley's gift clutched to her breasts. What in Blackwood's eyes made her tremble? Was it her first reaction to hearing his knock—believing he might be ready to confide in her about his nightmares? Or was it the something that had sparked between them?

She lifted the tiny garment to rub the delicate cotton against her cheek.

For long weeks she'd pondered Buckle's words concerning looking to the future. Now Serena fully realized what that might mean, and she wished for it above all else.

The Union

Matt hardly slept with all the feelings warring inside him. However, as he stared into the shaving mirror above the washstand, he was shocked to discover he didn't look tired, a new hope lit his eyes. The lackluster film of crushed hopes and broken dreams that had hung like a pall over him since he'd fallen in battle had begun to be lifted, and it was all due to Serena.

He breakfasted alone before reviewing the estate books once again. From what he'd been told yesterday, it was obvious he had too long let things drift here. If Serena hadn't seen what needed to be done, his tenants would have had good reason to be discontent. Instead, despite the cost of the improvements, the estate seemed to be more productive than ever. Serena's generosity had sparked a positive response in his people. He shook his head in wonder. Perhaps there was still a place for idealism, as long as one was prepared for reality to rear its inevitable head.

Serena. What other surprises would he discover about his bride? Considering, his heart gave one single stroke, bringing forth the odd stirrings and memories.

As if he could conjure her up, a soft knock sounded. Eagerly he called a greeting but was destined to disappointment.

"What a long face," Cecily gasped, one hand clutching her throat. "Is something wrong? Have you heard news from London? Not Father!"

The terror in her wide sherry eyes demanded reassurance.

"Poppet, it's nothing. I'm working too hard." He smiled, beckoning her to him. "Come and talk to me."

She took his hand, swinging it between them, as she perched on the edge of the dark walnut desk.

"I wanted to inform you of my plans. At the end of the week, if the weather holds, we shall lunch at the White Feathers and then view the ruin. As you requested, Serena is at work on a ball. This morning we put together the guest list. It's just wonderful how efficient Serena can be! Isn't she remarkable?" Cecily gushed.

His sister's objective was so transparent, Matt couldn't help smiling. The habit of cosseting his dramatic young sister was not easily broken.

"Yes, quite amazing. I hadn't realized when—"

"Well, how could you!" Cecily interrupted, her sherry eyes now flashing with indignation. "When you were ripped from her bosom on your wedding night! Thank goodness all that is at an end. We are all safe from that horrid Boney forever, and you and Kendall will never have to go to war again!"

For the first time, memory broke through the cool detachment he'd erected around his heart and mind. Suddenly he could feel Serena trembling against his shoulder; see her pink, temptingly soft lips part as his fingers slid through her hair, gently combing the thick, silken strands into a cascade of ebony across her throat and down over her round, full breasts.

The stirrings in his gut tightened to a hot ache and he recognized it for what it was—desire.

"Matt, are you all right?" Cecily asked, tugging on his sleeve, bringing him sharply back to reality.

"Yes, I was just thinking about the plans you've made. What does Kendall say?"

"Lord Kendall is enchanted." With a toss of her head, the dimple deepened in her cheek. "I shall make sure of that!"

The day dawned, cool but clear, as if it, too, were anxious to appease Lady Cecily. Kendall appeared pleased, his eyes sparkling green glints in the bright sunlight as he held his horse's head, gazing to where Cecily and Serena were engaged in a low conversation at the side of the drive.

Stepping toward them, Matt heard Serena say, "You know

I'm not a good—" before his sister looked up and saw him.

"Here is Matt!" she interrupted. "We should start now. I've taken care of everything," she added cryptically to Serena before moving to the mounting block.

"Good morning, my lord." Serena smiled a greeting. The strain between them had eased somewhat as they fell into the familiar routine of home. Suddenly a quick flash of fear appeared in her cornflower blue eyes as the grooms brought horses.

The instant he saw the brown mare meant for Serena, he guessed what his sister was up to. This horse was kept only for sentimental reasons. Cecily learned to ride on the gentle nag, who was devoid of either speed or stamina. Civility would demand Matt keep pace with Serena, thus allowing Cecily and Kendall to ride ahead.

"This horse won't do, Serena, she's much too docile. Bring a more spirited mount for her ladyship," he ordered the groom.

"Oh, no! I … I quite like the look of this horse!" Before Matt could stop her, she stepped forward and the groom tossed her into the saddle.

He sent a sharp, condemning look at his sister. He had to give her credit, she appeared utterly guileless as she sat her horse beside Kendall. However, his mood boded ill for her upon their return.

An hour out, as Matt had predicted, Serena's horse could not keep up with the other more spirited mounts. She apologized for slowing the pace but appeared perfectly happy to continue on. He admired the determined thrust to her chin and the glint in her eyes.

Matt finally called to Kendall and Cecily. "Go on ahead. We'll meet you there." Without hesitation, they galloped away, leaving him alone with his wife.

Her chin tilted even higher and Matt noticed how tightly she gripped the reins. "Blackwood, I know this must be shockingly slow going for your mount. I don't wish to spoil your ride."

Suddenly he realized she was not an experienced rider and had probably requested the easiest mount. It just proved how little he really knew about her.

"On the contrary, I welcome the opportunity to slow down. My leg still gives me twinges now and again," he lied gently, wanting to eradicate the strain in her eyes.

"Is it painful? If so, we should return to the Landing at once!"

"No, I believe if we continue to ride slowly, I should be fine."

Relief washed over her skin, bringing back healthy color as she nodded.

They had several miles to cover before they would reach the White Feathers. He was determined Serena should relax her grip upon the reins and enjoy the ride. So he began to talk about the countryside and the ruin they would be visiting after luncheon. He mentioned a book he'd recently discussed with the duke about the early Romans and was mildly surprised to discover she'd also read it. Books led to politics, to estate management, and suddenly they were discussing topics he'd never before spoken to a woman about. There seemed to be no topic that didn't burst into life as they shared their thoughts. Her grasp of what was happening on the continent and her questions about the congress taking place in Vienna stirred interests he thought lost forever. Before he was ready, the low inn loomed in front of them.

Cecily and Kendall were already seated before a crackling fire in the best parlor. They had ordered lunch and reported it should be served shortly.

Slipping down beside Cecily, Serena sent her a small smile. "You were right" she muttered, to his sister's giggling delight.

It was apparent to Matt, Serena was fully aware of Cecily's stratagems and was forgiving her deceptions. Or perhaps her deception was twofold: to steal some moments alone with Kendall and to protect Serena's reputation as a horsewoman. In any case, he had found the ride … enlightening. Those stirrings of new feelings that Serena inspired no longer were vague. He had picked up the thread of his new life.

And was in such a mellow mood that Cecily's sudden declaration that she had a shocking headache was accepted with no protest.

"Perhaps it was the mulled cider," she sighed dramatically. "I must rest. The three of you go on to the ruin without me."

"Can't say I'm that keen on it now. I'll stay and bear you company, Lady Cecily," Kendall declared gallantly.

"Oh, would you really, Lord Kendall? How very kind." Batting ridiculously long lashes, she gazed up at her brother. "I know Serena has been longing to view the ruin. You two go along without us. We'll wait here."

"Cecily, don't be a goose!" If he sounded prosy, he couldn't help it; some rules were utterly ingrained. "You know I can't leave you alone here with Kendall."

"Matt's right!" Kendall came to rigid attention. "I'll have the innkeeper's wife in to chaperon," he declared, coming to his senses.

True to his word, a few minutes later a comfortably round woman wearing a white apron and mobcap entered the parlor, curtsied, and took up a position in front of the fireplace.

"Mrs. Potter will stay until you return." Kendall smiled, his merry eyes dancing, and clasped Matt's shoulder. "You and Serena go ahead and enjoy yourself. I'll watch over your sister."

His sister was being sent a look from Serena that should have singed her curls, but Cecily merely gave another soulful sigh and peered up through her lashes into Kendall's face.

Matt, on the other hand, was feeling oddly in charity with his young sister. So much so, he had to feign sternness when a few minutes into their ride, Serena began to apologize.

"I fear Cecily is incorrigible, my lord. She means well, but is perhaps a trifle overzealous."

"Yes. I shall have to have a word with her," he declared firmly. "But let's not worry about Cecily now. There is the ruin ahead."

It faced the sea, with broken walls no longer invincible. Seabirds nested in its crannies, and weeds choked through the floor.

Matt took Serena's arm to help her over the uneven ground and was mildly surprised to realize the close contact quickened his pulse. Unbidden, once again, memories of their wedding night crashed over him. He was gratified when they reached the only standing tower where the floor was smooth. Serena stepped away.

"It's so quiet in here," she whispered, moving about the space to peer at faded mosaics still discernible upon the walls.

"The stones are high and thick, breaking the wind and the sound of the sea."

"Yes." She nodded, glancing up to where the roof should have been, but now the clear, cloudless sky and brilliant sun were visible. "It makes it quite warm here. Actually cozy."

"Rumor has it this is the favorite trysting spot for local lovers." His throat suddenly dry, he waited for her reaction.

It wasn't what he expected.

She laughed. "I can see this would be an excellent spot for boys to play. I wager you've spent several enjoyable hours here playing soldier and defending these wal—"

All color drained from her face, leaving the blue eyes, lit by glinting sunlight, blazing up at him with anguish.

"My lord, I…"

He quieted her by placing a fingertip over her soft lips, more determined to alleviate her distress than his own. "Shh, don't fret. You are correct." He lifted his finger, running it over her cheek, her color flowing back with his touch. "These were the first walls I defended. And, yes, they were happy hours."

She was so close to him and her cherry lips were parted so appealingly, he leaned toward her, drawn by her sweetness. Not because she was his wife, but because he wanted to take this unknown, vibrant woman into his arms.

Stepping back suddenly, she broke the spell. "My, it's grown cold." Folding her arms across her breasts, she shivered. "We should return to the inn and see to Cecily."

She was already moving back through the irregular opening; regretfully he followed.

In contrast to their ride earlier, a tense silence fell between them. Serena demanded Cecily ride slowly beside her all the way home so the headache would not be aggravated by a pounding gallop. Dutiful for once, Cecily complied.

The ride back was accomplished in comparative silence, but as he was preoccupied with his thoughts, the time went quickly for Matt.

Upon their return to the Landing, Cecily followed Matt into the library and shut the door behind them. With hands folded demurely, she stood before him. "I know I've been outrageous. I beg your forgiveness." With one of her dramatic sighs, she gazed solemnly up at him. "I am ready to accept my punishment."

Pinching her cold cheek gently, he laughed. "None of Her Grace's subtleties for you, hey, Poppet?"

"Really, Matt, you men are so slow at times. It's quite vexing!" Dimpling, she tossed her head, the white plume in her hat brushing her cheek. "Is my punishment complete?"

"Yes, if you answer me one question. Were your maneuvers to achieve time alone with Kendall or to force Serena and me to be alone?"

"Why, both, of course." She laughed, dancing out of the room with much of their mother's grace.

Staring after her, Matt smiled, oddly grateful.

In the days following their outing, Serena berated herself again and again. How could she have mentioned defending walls? Why had she brought up the very thing haunting him? It must be the bombardment of Fort McHenry that haunted his dreams. At night in the black stillness she could make out some of his words as he called orders to his men. If only he would share the nightmares with her, perhaps talking about them would rob them of power and they would cease to hold him in their grip.

Even though she berated herself, she still hugged that day tightly to her. Conversation had flowed so freely, as if there was nothing they couldn't discuss or find of interest to share. And there was that one moment in the warm quiet of the ruin when she'd literally ceased breathing. She'd broken the spell herself, fearful she was simply imagining his eyes held a new warmth as he looked at her.

By the night of the ball, she was trembling with anticipation whenever Blackwood was near. It wasn't the same excitement she'd felt so long ago when first she'd gazed up into his eyes. It was a deeper, secure feeling that her knowledge of his intelligence, his gentleness with his family, his continued generosity to his tenants, and his vulnerability engendered. The next time, she vowed, she'd not be the one to pull back. She would help him gather up his shattered idealism to form a pattern that once again would make him whole.

Dismissing her maid, Serena fussed in the mirror a moment more, tugging up on the plunging neckline of her blue silk gown. No doubt a habit she'd gotten from Buckle.

Without knocking, Cecily burst through the door. "Serena, your guests are arriving," she announced, twisting between her fingers one long curl which fell over her shoulder. "How do I look?" she fretted, peering into the mirror with an uncharacteristic frown marring her smooth forehead.

In a deep rose gown which showed off her beautiful long throat and rounded shoulders, Cecily was dazzling.

"Kendall won't be able to resist you," Serena reassured her.

"Well, he's doing a remarkably good job of it!" she declared, exasperation bringing added color to her cheeks. "Could I be any more obvious?"

"No!" Serena returned with real feeling. "Unless you plan to literally cast yourself at his feet."

"Well, there is that!" She laughed. "What do you plan next in your campaign with Matt?"

Anticipation and anxiety combined to make her insides one tight knot, but she ignored it to take Cecily in hand. "Come. We mustn't be late to receive our guests. As to my campaign with your brother, we shall simply have to see what the night will bring."

Lights and color and music swirled around her in the great hall as side by side she and Blackwood greeted their neighbors. The first time they'd been together at a ball, he'd been in full regimentals and she'd thought him a figure of heroic proportions. Now she knew he was so much more.

His black velvet jacket fit perfectly over his wide shoulders, and his ruffled evening shirt enhanced them. With a hiss of indrawn breath, she felt the knot tighten inside her as she remembered resting her cheek against his hard chest, the male scent of his skin, and his soft whispers which had made her feel safe and secure.

But the war had taken everything from her.

Refusing to dwell on the past, she carefully orchestrated the evening with a lifted brow to Stevens or a word to a footman when something needed attention. The great hall had never looked so festive. Even the tapestries hung against the walls, with their figures of huntsmen and hounds, seemed almost alive in the brilliant golden light.

The only flaw in her pleasure was receiving a note from Reverend Morton they would not be attending, for Mrs. Morton had come down with a shockingly bad head cold. Serena made a mental note to send a basket of sweets from the ball to the rectory in the morning.

Then all thought fled as Blackwood touched her arm and she looked up into those mesmerizing eyes.

"I believe we are expected to begin the dancing." With a shadow of his old whimsical smile, he took her hand and led her onto the floor.

His hand at her waist drawing her closer brought back a rush of memories: their first waltz, and that magical dance beside the reflection pool at Lady Sefton's when he'd declared he was asking for her hand on the morrow. Then, it had all been like a romantic dream. Now, if he reached out to her so, it would have so much more substance, for she had grown to realize not only his true worth but her own.

As always, their steps were perfectly matched, and with a catch of happiness, she realized his leg was completely healed. If only all else could be.

The waltz was barely finished when their neighbor, Sir Henry Winston, claimed her hand. Blackwood gave her a smile of regret as Sir Henry led her into a country dance. Once again she thought she glimpsed golden glints of a new warmth in his eyes.

The evening conspired to keep them apart, although often their eyes met across the width of the room. Which was perhaps as well, for the knot inside her was nearly painful when he was near. It was as if she was holding her breath in anticipation. She refused to admit what she now yearned to happen between them, for she knew events did not always fall into place as desired.

After supper Serena was making her way to thank the chef for his brilliant effort when in the entry hall she spied Stevens scolding little Polly Brown, who stood before him, shivering, with tears running down her red cheeks.

"What's going on here?" she demanded, rushing forward. Polly burst into tears and Serena knelt beside her. "Polly, why are you here so late?" she asked gently, taking the frozen little fingers in her warm ones.

"It be Ma," she sobbed. "The babe's comin' early. Pa went after the midwife. She be visitin' her sister up the coast. He sent me to the rectory, but the parson's gone and his missus is laid up. I didn't know what to do so, I came here ... There's somethin' wrong this time. There's so much blood," she whispered, her eyes round with terror. "I don't know how to help Ma."

"Polly, don't cry. I shall come with you to help your mother." Still holding the little fingers, Serena stood. "Stevens, order the carriage at once, and fetch my cloak."

If Serena suddenly declared she was flying to the moon, he couldn't have been more thunderstruck. "But, my lady. You have guests," he gasped. "Let me send one of the maids."

The little fingers tightened around her hand, and Polly gazed up with tear-reddened, trusting eyes.

"I shall deal with this myself. My guests are having a marvelous time and shall continue to do so with or without my presence. Now, please hurry. Mrs. Brown needs attention."

With stiff disapproval he snapped his fingers to two waiting footmen, and her cloak and carriage were instantly produced.

"Please inform Lord Blackwood and Lady Cecily what has occurred, but don't cause undue alarm."

He looked so pained, she immediately realized she'd

insulted him. "Of course, I know I can count on you to do the proper thing, Stevens," she added with what she hoped was a soothing smile.

She had no time for more. Obviously Mrs. Brown needed help.

How much help brought cold terror to clasp around Serena's heart. The small space the Browns used for their bedchamber was taken up nearly all by a bed. Mrs. Brown lay in a pool of blood seeping into the covers.

Her pain-filled eyes widened in shock. "My lady, you shouldn't be here." Gasping for air, she tried to struggle up to her elbows. "Not proper you being here."

Kneeling beside the bed, Serena stopped her with a gentle hand on her shoulder. "Rest, Mrs. Brown. I will try to make you more comfortable until the midwife arrives."

With a harsh intake of breath, she nodded. "It not be like the other babes."

"I know. Try to relax. I'll return in a moment."

Stepping through the narrow doorway, she glanced up and saw seven little faces peering down at her from the loft. Polly stood by the fireplace twisting her hands together.

"Polly, boil water and gather fresh linens."

The little girl instantly flew around the room to do her bidding.

Serena sent John Coachman back to the Landing with instructions to fetch more linens and a maid, for another pair of hands might be needed.

Then she tied an apron over her impractical gown and carried hot water and linens back into the tiny chamber.

Mrs. Brown sighed, muttering her thanks as Serena staunched the flow of blood as best she could, cleansed, and replaced the sodden linen with fresh. She was placing a cool cloth on Mrs. Brown's hot forehead when the midwife finally arrived.

With one quick glance, she nodded. "Aye, your ladyship did right well. I'll take over now."

"I'll leave you in the midwife's capable hands," Serena whispered, squeezing Mrs. Brown's limp fingers.

Twisting her head, she spoke so softly, Serena had to bend low to hear. "You be a great lady" came through cracked, dry lips.

With a last squeeze to the hand, Serena took her leave. Stepping out, she found Daniel Brown standing near the fire with Polly. Their faces were identical in fear.

She wanted to reassure them. "Mr. Brown, I'm sure—"

"Your ladyship, quick! I need you!" the midwife cried, and Serena rushed back to the bedside.

"It be bad. Hemorrhaging." The weathered old face was grim, the watery eyes staring at her appraisingly. "If I'm to save the babe, I need help. Can you do it?"

"Just tell me what must be done," Serena returned with equal grimness.

Time ceased to exist as she did what the midwife instructed, applying pressure where it was needed, holding Mrs. Brown's thrashing, pain-racked body, keeping up the supply of linens and hot water, all their efforts focused on saving the baby and Mrs. Brown.

But in the end, their efforts weren't enough.

The midwife placed a wrapped bundle in Serena's arms. "Daniel has another daughter."

"Mrs. Brown?" Serena asked through a tight burning in her throat.

The midwife shook her head. "Best send Daniel in."

Serena had been so young when her mother died, she didn't have any memory of death; now, to see its mark left her with a deep sadness which settled into her chest like a cold lump and lodged there.

Holding the sleeping infant, Serena passed through the narrow doorway to find Daniel hovering outside.

"You have a daughter," she whispered.

"Aye. Can I go in now?" he asked quickly.

At her nod, he brushed past her. An instant later she heard his hoarse cries. The cold lump inside her expanded.

Polly sat on the low couch by the hearth, tears washing her pale cheeks with red streaks. Serena carefully placed the baby in her arms. "You have a new sister."

Nodding, she glanced at the baby and then up at Serena. "Ma's dead, ain't she?" she whispered hoarsely.

Slipping down beside her, Serena placed her hand over the small ones clutching the bundle to her. "Yes, Polly. But she will always be in your heart."

"No!" she sobbed, her little chest heaving with her pain. "I need my ma here with me! We all do!"

Gathering the child close, she let the little face rest against the bodice of her ruined gown as she stroked the fine hair.

"I lost my mother when I was a little girl, but my father taught me she was always there if I wished. Close your eyes, Polly."

With a hiccup, she obeyed.

"Can you see your mother?"

"No," she moaned between sobs.

"Look really hard and she'll be there." Serena swallowed a lump in her throat. "Do you see her now? What is she doing?"

"She's baking gingerbread cakes," Polly whispered, tears squeezing from beneath her tightly closed lids. "It be Christmas and it smells so good cause Ma's baking us gingerbread cakes and we kids are settin' at the table waitin' impatient-like. She be smilin' at us."

"What a beautiful memory." Serena rested her cheek against the small head. "When you're sad or lonely, or whenever you need her, you must simply close your eyes and she'll be there. Smiling at you."

Her own eyes burning with tears, she blinked and looked up. Through the watery haze she found Blackwood standing in the doorway, staring at her with an expression she'd never seen before.

For some reason, that look cracked the cold lodged in her chest into a thousand splinters. Resting her cheek again upon the silken strands, she wept with all her own pain.

Never before in Matt's life had he felt such tenderness. It filled every muscle and sinew, knitting him into wholeness. He'd rushed here after giving Stevens a tongue-lashing for not informing him immediately of Serena's intention. Now to find her holding Polly in her arms, creating such beauty and strength out of such tragedy, made him ashamed of his own inability to do the same.

Striding into the room, he knelt beside her. "I've brought the maid and the linens you requested."

Looking up, her cornflower eyes brilliant with tears, she shook her head. "It's too late."

"Yes. But there's still much to be done. You have done your duty. Now I must do mine."

Returning to the door, he issued orders to John Coachman to fetch Mrs. Watley here at once. She wished someone to care for, and now the Brown children needed her caring. Turning to the maid, he commanded her to take charge until morning. He was glad she was older and mature, not one of the flighty ones. He was reassured when, without hesitation, she removed her cloak, folded it neatly on a chest, and climbed the ladder to check on the sleeping Brown children who would awake to find themselves motherless.

Turning back, he found Serena had coaxed Polly up and they were laying the baby in the wooden cradle next to the fire.

"Mrs. Watley will be here to help you, Polly. And the maid from the Landing will spend the night. But I must take her ladyship home."

Her little face, red and swollen with crying, looked up at him and nodded.

He was beginning to recognize the determined thrust of Serena's chin, but he wouldn't be put off. She looked ready to drop from fatigue.

"I be fine, my lady," Polly said in a hoarse little voice, persuading Serena more surely than Matt could have done. "My ma's here with me just like you told me. All I do is close my eyes and she be smilin' at me."

The firelight caught the glistening tears on Serena's cheeks as she leaned forward, hugging Polly tightly to her and kissing the top of her head.

"I shall be back. I promise."

Before Serena could protest, Matt had enveloped her in her cloak, whisked her outside, and put her up before him on his horse. He settled Serena, one arm holding her tightly to him.

"Close your eyes and I shall have you home in no time."

And in truth the ride through the clear, cold night was on wings. Again, as on the outing to the ruin, their journey ended before he was ready to release Serena from his arms.

To his delight he discovered he didn't have to let her go, for she'd fallen into an exhausted sleep. Although he tried to shift her gently as they came to a halt at the side door, her eyelids fluttered open.

"Are we home?"

"Yes. We're going in the back way so I can take you straight to your bedchamber."

He leapt down and swept her off the horse and into his arms. Striding past a stunned maid at the side door, he barked an order. "Send Lady Cecily to Lady Blackwood at once!"

She bolted to do his bidding. This night he'd been uncharacteristically sharp with the servants, which would no doubt be the talk of the hall tomorrow. He would make amends. But nothing else mattered now except getting his exhausted wife safely into her bed.

"Blackwood, truly you shouldn't. I can certainly walk," she protested, but with none of her usual spirit.

"Yes, I know. But indulge me." Reaching her bedchamber, he opened the door and kicked it shut behind him.

A ghost of a smile curled her mouth. "I thought this sort of behavior only occurred in novels. Truly you may put me down now."

This time he complied, slowly lowering Serena to the floor. For just an instant she leaned into him, her palms flat against his chest as she regained her balance. With his hands still at her waist, he lowered his head, unable to resist her another moment.

The door crashed open and he jerked back, startled.

"Serena! Are you all right? The maid said you were being carried to your bedchamber!" Cecily declared, her eyes wide with fear.

A flush colored Serena's pale cheeks. "I'm just exhausted, that's all."

He could hear it in her voice. With reluctance he realized now was not the time to explore his feelings, which could no longer be repressed.

"I'll leave you then." Unable to resist at least one touch, he lifted her hand to his lips. "Rest well, Serena. We shall talk in the morning."

He was rewarded with a wavering smile and a nod.

That was enough to fire him with an excitement he hadn't felt in a very long time. He paced back and forth across the carpet of his chamber, staring at the door separating them.

After what seemed like hours, he knocked softly. As he expected, his sister answered.

"She's asleep," Cecily whispered, motioning him in.

Going to the bed, they both stared down at her sleep-flushed face against the white pillowcase, her ebony curls spilling around her.

"She told me what happened. Poor Serena! What a terrible tragedy to witness." Cecily's young face was marked with sadness. "She must have been terrified!"

"She was magnificent." Regardless of his sister's presence, he lifted one ebony curl in his fingers, rubbing its texture through his fingers.

"Should I stay with her in case she wakes?" Cecily whispered, touching his arm.

"No, I shall leave the connecting door open so I can hear if she needs anything."

Before he left, he built up the fire so a bright glow lit her room. If she woke during the night and needed anything, she wouldn't be in darkness.

He lay in his own bed for a long time, listening, but she slept soundly.

Witnessing her indomitable strength, her courage at such a tragic time, her tender offering of hope to the child, had relit some of his old idealism. The world was not a perfect place. No one should expect that. But life went on. And in the response to the tragedies and hurts, as well as the triumphs, true character was formed.

Tomorrow he would search out his answers and devise a new direction. One that would bring him to Serena...

A shout woke her.

The instant she sat up, she saw the open door and knew Blackwood was again trapped in his nightmare.

After all that had happened tonight, she couldn't turn away from him and ignore his needs. She feared the agony he must be suffering more than she feared his rejection.

The bright firelight cast into relief his wide, firmly muscled chest tapering to narrow hips. As she'd done before, she leaned into him, using her weight to help her grip the twisting shoulders in her hands.

"Matt, please wake up. Matt, please!" A sob in her voice, she leaned closer. No more pain tonight. For any of them. "Matt, wake up and it will end!"

His eyes flew open, the pupils expanding to study her face as intently as if for the first time.

"Serena, you're here," he breathed with such tenderness, she began to tremble.

"You're cold," he exclaimed, gathering her closer until she was spooned against his warmth.

Her heart pounded so loudly, surely he could feel it where her breasts pressed against his arm? Afraid to speak, to do anything to break this spell, she willed her pulse to calm.

"I'm sorry I woke you again. Someday I shall talk about the nightmares. Then perhaps I can vanquish them."

With a courage that had been forged this night, she shifted so she rested on his chest to study his face in the glow from the hearth. 'Tell me. Together, we can surely vanquish them."

A light sparked in the dark eyes. "You've been through so much tonight, I—"

This time it was she who stopped him with gentle fingers on his lips.

"Above all else, I wish to share your pain."

Clasping her fingers, he pressed a kiss on their tips and then held them tightly.

"My nightmares are of the two days my regiment was ripped

to pieces. I was powerless to do anything." A faraway look came into his eyes and Serena knew he was back amongst his men. "Higgens fell. Even though the men fought bravely, there was no hope. I tightened our line, encouraging the men. For the first time, ever, I felt despair. That's when I scribbled my farewell to you. Then I was wounded, trapped beneath my dead horse, but they rallied to me. My own men, forming a shield around me. Even Jeffries. And for what?"

He shut his eyes and Serena felt his chest heave with remembered pain.

"The battle shifted, but Jeffries wouldn't leave me. He was always so damn stubborn! He was shot through the heart trying to drag me to safety.

"It was all utterly meaningless." As he opened his eyes upon her face, his voice roughened. "All those deaths! A needless waste of brave men's lives. We were at the peace table, but we had our orders. Fight on! For what? I once thought I knew. But as I lay there with Jeffries's lifeblood oozing over me, I realized I didn't know anything. I had only been an idealistic dreamer seeing all as I wished, not as it was. My world and the people in it became strangers to me."

Swallowing back tears at the anguish tightening the skin against the strong bones of his face, she found her answer in honesty. "I was a stranger. You thought me perfect, and when you returned, you saw I was not. Had never been. Plus I had changed in truth and became … me. I'm sorry, but I'm not sure perfection is possible for any of us."

He gripped her shoulders so tightly, they ached as he held her firmly to him. "Serena, you are…" He shook his head, his eyes boring into her. "There are no words to describe what I felt when I saw you with Polly, heard your words. Such strength and understanding humbles me. You are…"

"I am your wife," she finished for him. The force that had driven her along this path since his return took another twist, and for the first time, she initiated an embrace. This night she needed to be held in these arms again. And in his eyes she saw an answering need.

She touched her lips in slow movements over his wrinkled brow until it smoothed, down over the strong cheeks to the long mouth, and hovered there. "I'm your wife, Matt." For the first time she used his name freely.

Cupping the back of her head with a grip of steel, he pulled her mouth down to his, letting her feel the warmth of his desire. She met the scorching passion with her own aching needs.

His mouth took hers again and again as they strained to be closer. His deft fingers slid her night-shift down her body so there was nothing stopping their desperation to touch and be touched.

In the dim light her gaze found his mesmerizing eyes bright with passion. He placed his hands on either side of her face and levered himself up.

"Serena, perfection has a new meaning, and it is you."

"No, my dearest, it is us—together."

Through the onslaught of dizzying emotion she rejoiced he did not speak of love, for he had the first time, and that was as nothing to what she felt now. He filled her with such exquisite sensations, she was not lost to passion, she became one with it.

At last she slept nestled against him, her cheek resting upon his heart, the steady beat bringing her peace.

Somewhere in the fuzziness of half sleep she thought she heard a knock and a voice and stirred fretfully. But he quieted her with a whisper and she felt his lips playing across her curls. Everything was all right now. They had a new beginning.

From somewhere deep in her sleep-numbed mind fear woke, but she pushed it back to its dark corner, clasping her husband more tightly in her arms.

The Separation

1815

Sometime during the night they shifted position; Serena was no longer resting her cheek against Matt's chest, nor could she hear the strong, even beat of his heart. But she could hear his voice repeating her name over and over again. To respond she must brush aside the cobwebs of sleep and open her eyes.

He was sitting beside her on the edge of the bed, but with a jolt that brought her fully awake, she realized he was in traveling clothes.

"Matt, is it your father?" she asked with real alarm, fearing the worst.

"No, Serena," he answered quickly, taking her hands with a numbing grip. "Long arrived last night with news from the Continent."

The fear that she'd pushed back into its dark corner rushed forth, bringing her scrambling up to kneel before him. Dreading the answer, nonetheless she forced herself to ask. "What is it?"

"Napoleon is on the march, gathering an army behind him. The Duke of Wellington has gone to Brussels, where he's to command the allied troops to meet the French. He particularly requested me on his staff."

His words reached her, but they made no sense. He would think her dull-witted, even at such an early hour and after such a night as they had shared. As she stared into his face, the look in his dark eyes was too complex to read. "I don't understand."

"Serena, you must understand it is my duty to go," Matt said gently.

"You can't mean it!" she cried, her heart pounding through

her with such force, she trembled. When he didn't speak, she answered herself. "No, of course you don't mean it. Not after the nightmares. Not after the senseless loss of your men. Of Higgens. Of Jeffries. Not after all you've suffered!"

He was as pale as the white marble fireplace, but his eyes blazed so dark, they appeared black.

"Serena, you have helped me to find myself. To accept. You are correct. I no longer see war through the eyes of that idealistic youth. I know it is neither glorious nor noble. But it is sometimes necessary."

He was breathing as quickly as she was, but his voice was calm and firm. "Because of your courage and understanding, I have come to accept that, regardless of everything else, I am a soldier. A soldier who must do what is honorable and just. It is honorable and just to stop Napoleon once and for all. And that I must do."

Not again! Just as they were beginning, they would be separated! All the fear and uncertainty! Not again!

At last the pain was more than she could bear. She ripped her hands from his warm grasp, recoiling back until the headboard bit into her spine.

"Then last night meant nothing to you! I mean nothing to you." The tears stood, burning, on her face. Suddenly her voice was raw with desperation. "You would leave me again because your honor is more important than what we share?"

He was standing quite still, and she saw him literally cease breathing. "This is who I am," he went on with obvious difficulty. "My honor is as much a part of me as my feelings for you are. Last night I saw you confront tragedy with something of beauty and strength. I can do no less. Nor would you wish me to. When I return—"

"No! Don't bother!" she cried, unable to hold rational thought in the maelstrom of pain. "Go to your stupid honorable war. Get killed yourself! I won't be waiting like a stupid fool this time!"

Putting both hands over her face, she wept, coiled in a tight ball of fear and confusion.

"Sweetheart, please listen."

She heard the desperate plea in his voice, and when he touched her shoulder, she dropped her hands and opened her eyes.

"Don't call me that and don't touch me," Serena whispered through the agony in her throat. "Leave me! I don't care if I ever lay eyes on you again!"

A chill spread through her nerves and flesh as, dry-eyed, she watched him leaving for the last time.

It seemed like an eternity that she stared blindly at the door he closed between them. She couldn't quite form her thoughts into any logical pattern. In a handful of hours she'd helped bring a child into the world, witnessed a woman's death, and for the first time in nearly two years, spent a magical time in her husband's arms, only to awaken to find him leaving her once again. She had a right to be exhausted, frightened, sick at heart, and confused, didn't she?

The confusion stilled for an instant to mark one undeniable truth: Matt was leaving to face God knew what, and she'd sent him on his way with the memory of angry words.

Stumbling off the bed, she called his name and pulled open the door. In a state of shocking dishabille she ran, barefoot, toward the staircase. Through the tall mullion window she caught a glimpse of Matt and Kendall as they rode away.

If she hadn't caught the back of one of the fragile gilt chairs lined up against the wall, she would have crumpled to the carpet. Instead she fell onto the low satin cushion and buried her head on her lap.

Cecily found her there, still weeping, and joined her, kneeling beside the chair.

"Oh, Serena, they're gone!" she sobbed, their curls tangling together upon one another's shoulders. "I should have thrown myself literally at Kendall's feet. At least I would have had something."

Breathing hurt her tight, tear-congested chest, but Serena took a deep breath and gripped Cecily's shoulders, holding her at arm's length. "Surely you know Kendall cares for you, Cecily.

You have that."

Nodding, her little face crumpled like a child's. "I know. And Matt cares for you. Last night ... something happened between you, didn't it? I can see it in your eyes."

"Yes, let's all discuss Matt and Serena's love life," Longford drawled, suddenly looming over them. "The two footmen at the bottom of the stairs are getting an earful, plus stiff necks from trying to peer up here for a peek of your loveliness, Serena. Cecily, go fetch her robe," he commanded, flicking both girls a bored glance.

"You're a beast!" Cecily snapped, but ran nonetheless to the bedchamber.

Waiting, Serena folded her arms across her scantily clad bosom, and stared at the floor.

"This is certainly not the woman who singlehandedly changed the face of Avalon Landing. The woman who overnight has become a veritable angel to the entire country," he mocked in his old, hated way.

Striving to maintain some kind of composure, Serena was saved by Cecily's prompt return with her robe.

Holding it tightly around her, Serena rose and faced him with lifted chin. "Longford, Cecily is correct. You are a beast. It is my fondest wish that when your tiny heart is finally given, the lady crumbles it to dust."

Placing a protective arm about Serena's shoulders, Cecily nodded. "Yes, Long, it's as much as you deserve for being so insensitive. We are desolate at being separated from our loved ones. Surely you must realize that!"

"Then have the good manners to be desolate in private and not involve me! I've too much to do to deal with it!" Folding his arms across his dusty riding jacket, he studied them from under his hooded lids. "I came up here to tell both of you I must leave immediately. Matt has requested I find him ten good horses and ship them to the Continent. I suggest the both of you return to London with me. News will arrive more quickly there, and Their Graces will want you close."

"An excellent idea, Longford," Serena agreed, trying to

gather some semblance of order in her chaotic thoughts. "However, I can't leave until after Mrs. Brown's funeral and I have made final arrangements for help from Mrs. Watley for the Brown children."

If she could feel anything but numb horror at all that had happened, she would have been surprised by his accommodating nod.

"Two days. And then we're for London!"

London was not the haven of peace where Serena could sort through her confusion and decide what to do about her marriage. For certainly something had to be done, but just what wasn't clear.

The house was one of illness, where everything revolved around the duke's declining health. London itself was in the grips of another Season, but one quite out of the ordinary, for half the *ton* was missing.

"Town's dull as dishwater. The whole world has gone to Brussels," Aunt Lavinia stated flatly, fanning herself while Serena poured tea.

"So I've rented a house. Lucky to get one, I'm such a late-comer. Frederick escorts me tomorrow. Heard tell your husband's gone to join Wellington. Why didn't you accompany him? Everything all right and tight between the two of you?" she asked, finally revealing the reason for her unexpected visit.

Her owl eyes slitted, studying Serena in that particular way which she found a trifle unnerving given the state of her mind.

Her father would be thoroughly shocked and saddened if he knew how easily she was learning to tell falsehoods.

"Aunt Lavinia, Blackwood and I are unexceptional. He left so quickly, there was no question of my accompanying him."

"Well, I'll be there. Always a place for you if you decide to come. Should, you know. Nothing going on here."

For once, Aunt Lavinia was correct. Without a ball or musical or soiree every day, Cecily had nothing to divert her mind from missing Kendall. Her woebegone little face even brought a reprimand from Her Grace, who informed her daughter she should take her example from Serena by putting a brave face on a difficult situation.

Just how difficult, no one knew. They had no idea it was now Serena who awoke at night in the sway of reliving that final morning with Matt. Over and over she heard herself say the hurtful words. She didn't understand why he'd acted as he had. Any more than she understood how she could have so forgotten herself to give vent to her feelings.

The arrival of her father for a visit to the duke's sickbed was a welcome relief, particularly since he brought Buckle. But not even to her beloved nursemaid did she reveal how quickly her life had plummeted from magical to miserable.

Only Longford's declaration that he was leaving for Brussels in two days brought Serena out of her daze of confused misery.

"Why?" she asked boldly, meeting his mocking gaze without a flinch across the dining table. "What is going on?"

"Yes, Richard. This decision is rather surprising considering the duke's health," the duchess remarked from the head of the table.

Cecily leaned forward to gaze at her brother in rapt attention. She hadn't missed the surprisingly sharp note in the duchess's usually melodic voice.

Even Papa peered at the marquess over the top of his glasses.

Only Buckle, who had been asked to join them since they dined *en famille*, sat quietly with hands folded, her gaze on Serena.

"Well, Richard?" the duchess prompted. "Politics has never interested you before."

"It does now!" he stated in a deep voice with nothing of boredom in it. "There must be a final confrontation between the allies and Napoleon. It could change the face of history."

"And you believe you might be able to assist?" his mother asked gently.

"Good God, mother, I've found a way my humdrum existence might hold some meaning! If you must know, I'm carrying dispatches from the War Office. Perhaps I've misunderstood your subtleties over the years. I believed you would approve."

"I simply desired to know your true intention." The duchess looked steadily into her son's identical eyes. "Now that you have made them clear, I see that you must go."

"I'm going with you! I can stay with Aunt Lavinia," Serena heard herself declaring, suddenly seeing a path open to make desperately needed amends with Matt.

"I'm going, too," Cecily chimed in, leaping to her feet. "If there is to be a confrontation, I must see Kendall!"

Longford stared at them in horror. "You're both mad! I have no intentions of playing nursemaid to the pair of you all the way to Brussels!"

"Excuse me, my lord, if I may," Buckle broke in, shocking them all to silence. "If Serena and Lady Cecily wish to accompany you to the Continent, I would be happy to go as their companion so you wouldn't be bothered by any of their needs."

"What an excellent idea," the duchess sighed, casting Buckle a look of quiet respect. "If it were not for His Grace's health, I would go myself. But with you attending the girls, their accompanying him will cause Longford no difficulty whatsoever."

"Hmpt."

All eyes turned to Serena's father as he cleared his throat. "Mrs. Buckle, are you quite sure you are up to such a long journey?"

Buckle gave him her singularly sweet smile. "Quite sure. As long as you're able to manage without me in my absence."

Reverend Fitzwater peered over the rim of his glasses first at Buckle, then the duchess, lingered a moment on Longford and Cecily, and came to rest on Serena. From what she saw in that steady gaze, she knew she hadn't kept her heartsickness over Matt as much a secret as she'd hoped.

"Considering everything"—he spoke with a firm calmness, much as he did from the pulpit—"I see no reason why Lady Cecily and Serena, with Buckle as companion, should not visit Brussels. I know my sister will welcome them. That is, of course, if the marquess is agreeable."

There was nothing of calmness in Longford's abrupt push to his feet or the cold look he inflicted on his mother, Cecily, and Serena in turn.

"The dispatches will be ready the day after tomorrow. I leave then, with or without you!" he declared grimly, before turning on his heels and striding from the room.

Never had there been a flurry of activity to match their efforts to assemble and pack for what might be a lengthy stay in Brussels. Serena surreptitiously tucked a few extra medical supplies in her bandbox, just in case.

Brussels was gayer than London at the height of the Season, so ball gowns, riding clothes, walking costumes, all must be carefully packed in tissue for their journey.

Serena worked like one possessed, for she was determined to hasten their leave-taking. Each moment away from Matt reinforced her hated words "Leave me! I don't care if I ever lay eyes on you again!"

She must see him. Tell him she still didn't understand why he left her, but she hadn't meant to say all she did. It was the pain and fear that caused her to lash out so. She'd felt so safe, so content in his arms. To be ripped from them once again was more than she could bear.

She had to confront him with all that lay between them: all the misunderstandings and misconceptions, all the words they should have said but had never spoken to one another.

Buckle's sweet calmness was their salvation as Longford drove them relentlessly to the coast, where the yacht waited to cross the Channel to Belgium.

They arrived at Lady Charlesworth's in the early hours of a warm June morning. The entire household went into an uproar.

After promising to send Matt as soon as he found him, Longford practically dumped them on the doorstep with all their luggage and left to go to allied headquarters. The butler, a very superior little man, appeared scandalized, but the three women were so exhausted, they couldn't have cared less.

"All I wish for is a bed," Cecily moaned, closing her eyes, leaning against Buckle's shoulder.

"And that you shall have," Buckle promised in the tone Serena vaguely remembered from the nursery.

By the time a maid roused Aunt Lavinia from her slumber, Buckle had them settled in a small parlor and went to the kitchen to fetch hot chocolate herself.

"You're here!" Aunt Lavinia gasped, her owl eyes slitted in weighed fatigue. "Who brought you? Surely Mrs. Buckle wasn't your only chaperon," she demanded, falling into a chair.

Mrs. Buckle promptly placed a cup in her limp hands.

"Drink this, Lady Charlesworth. It should restore you. The Marquess of Longford escorted us here."

"Longford here, too! Is he also to be my houseguest?"

Although fatigue was making her so dull that every time she blinked, her lids opened increasingly slower, Serena forced her eyes wide to confront her aunt.

"I assumed your kind offer that there was always room for me was heartfelt. And would surely extend to my family."

"Serena, you sound like your sainted papa," Aunt Lavinia yawned, pushing herself to her feet. "Of course you're all welcome. Longford, too, if he chooses. For a rental, the house is snug. You and Cecily can have the two rooms across from mine. Mrs. Buckle will take the room allocated for the governess. Should I call a footman to carry the child?"

Shaking her head, Serena nudged Cecily awake. She opened her eyes, and allowed Serena and Buckle to help her to stand, swaying with fatigue between them.

"Best get her to bed," Aunt Lavinia commanded. "I suggest you all get some rest. You shall want to look your best for the Duchess of Richmond's ball tonight. Everyone who's anyone shall be in attendance."

Matt would be there. If Longford didn't bring him sooner, Serena would see him at the ball. Perhaps he could explain to her so she could understand why he continued this thing that had caused him so much pain and loss. And in turn she would tell him what she'd never said aloud before.

That thought kept her going, making her exhausted slumber sweeter with dreams.

With Buckle's help, they left for the Duchess of Richmond's ball confident they looked their best, Cecily in a demure white gown with a deep ruffle at the hem, and Serena in her favorite cornflower blue with matching ribbons threaded through her curls.

The duchess greeted them warmly at her rented house in the Rue de la Blanchisserie. "It seems all of the *ton* is in Brussels. For this Season, soldiers are the fashion."

Soldiers. Their striking red jackets and gold epaulets stood out starkly in the ground-floor ballroom hung with the royal colors of crimson, gold, and black.

Even though Aunt Lavina swiftly made her way through the throng, Serena, with Cecily at her side, moved slowly, her gaze searching for just one dark-haired soldier with deep, unfathomable eyes.

Finally taking a position near a pillar wreathed in ribbons, bows, and flowers, Serena had an excellent view of the wide, rectangular doors so she could miss none who entered.

The wail of the bagpipes filled the room as the Highlanders performed the fling. Something in the mournful quality of the pipes brought such sadness, Serena had to swallow back a lump in her throat.

Then the musicians in the gallery above broke into his music an instant before Wellington himself appeared and the Duchess of Richmond quickly crossed the floor to greet him.

Serena's heartbeat was so loud and painful, she had to take deep, even breaths to calm it. Where was Matt? She must see him! There was something in the very air that demanded desperate action. It was like a wild summer storm brewing all around them. She could feel its power, but was powerless herself to stop whatever might come.

Cecily had been oddly quiet, refusing to dance, until at last Kendall appeared in the doorway, candlelight turning his crisp, sandy curls to copper. She moved a step forward, but his eyes found her and he quickly made his way to them.

"Couldn't believe it when Longford tracked me down and told me you were here!" Bowing, he took Serena's hand, squeezing it. "Sorry Matt isn't with me. The duke sent him out early this morning to discover what's happened to his usually excellent secret service. Haven't heard from the scouts in days."

Serena froze with bitter disappointment, but forced her lips into a smile. "I shall simply have to be patient. But we are delighted to see you, Kendall."

"Yes, delighted," Cecily breathed, extending both her hands.

With bright dancing eyes, Kendall lifted them to his lips. "If you'll excuse us, Serena, I believe this is my waltz with Lady Cecily."

Cecily had never looked more beautiful than when Kendall swept her into his arms and they twirled around the room. It was almost painful to watch the adoration on her innocent face.

Serena now understood what war could mean; she'd heard it in Matt's nightmares and seen it on his face when he told her of his loss. The excitement growing all around struck terror in her heart. If, as Longford predicted, there must be one great confrontation, many men in this room would not return from it. Even Kendall. Or Matt.

Trembling with sick terror, Serena stared blindly around, blocking out everything, willing Matt to appear.

Finally the whispers that began with an officer in Prussian black rushing into the ballroom, the dust of travel still clinging to him, penetrated even through her numbness.

"…Napoleon has crossed the border with his entire army at Charleroi … two hundred thousand men … one million men … Picton to march to Quatre Bras…" The whispers grew louder and louder as dancers began to leave the floor. A large crowd formed around the duke, who remained almost stoically calm.

Swiftly Kendall brought Cecily back to her. "I must go. Don't worry. We'll rout Boney once and for all this time." He grinned with a confidence that brought the ache of tears to Serena's eyes.

"Lord Kendall, do you remember kissing me when I was fourteen?" Cecily asked, a thread of desperation in her voice.

Kendall's dancing eyes widened. "Lady Cecily, surely not!" he gasped in mock horror. Another slow grin curved his mouth.

"Now that I think of it, I have a very vague memory of your pigtail. Quite charming if I recall."

"Then I shall have to give you an even clearer memory to take with you."

With that, she stood on tiptoes and pressed a firm kiss on Kendall's mouth. Hastily Cecily stepped back, her face scarlet, her lips quivering in a smile. "So you won't forget me."

The green eyes were suddenly very serious as Kendall lifted Cecily's hand and placed a kiss in her palm.

"I assure you, Lady Cecily, to forget you is impossible."

He spun on his heels, disappearing into the stream of red flowing out the door.

The storm was breaking all around them. Reaching out, Serena tightly clasped Cecily's hand.

"What does it mean?" Cecily asked with tears running down her cheeks.

With a certainty that burned her insides like acid, Serena knew she wouldn't have the moment with Matt Cecily had just stolen with Kendall, for there was no time left, for any of them.

"It has begun," she whispered, closing her eyes against the pain.

It had begun and they should have known, but didn't, Matt raged, driving his horse faster to reach Wellington with the news his secret service had failed utterly. Instead of attacking around his right to cut him off from the sea, Bonaparte had chosen to march through Belgium and attempt to drive a wedge between the British and Dutch troops and the Prussians.

"Napoleon has humbugged me, by God!" Wellington remarked.

Matt stood at attention, hardly daring to move when the commander was in this mood.

"Blackwood, you must ride out again." Opening his ever-present portfolio of pen, ink, and paper, he scribbled orders. "Deliver this to Picton. We can't take the French at Quatre Bras. But we must hold them as long as possible."

A fresh horse eager beneath him, Matt spared a moment of gratitude to his brother for procuring him such fine horseflesh. With thoughts of home came Serena's parting words to haunt him. He shook his head, rejecting everything but what lay ahead.

Quatre Bras must not be taken.

He presented the orders to Picton, who, cursing, rammed his black top hat more firmly upon his head. "Ney attacked at two while we shilly-shallied around cooking breakfast; the day was almost lost. But we're here, by God! And we'll hold. Blackwood, inform the infantry they must stand to a man."

Riding between the infantry squares, Matt shouted orders. When he couldn't be heard, he gestured, making sure the men understood. At the second cavalry charge his horse was shot from under him. Rolling off to safety, he scrambled to his feet and ran, dodging bullets, to where a French cavalry horse stood, his rider dead, tangled in the reins at his forelock.

He shoved the body aside and leapt on. He dug his spurs sharply into the horse's sides, for he had the most forward regiment to alert. Thank God it was Kendall's so they recognized him even on a horse with French insignia. The front rank lowered their bayonets and the second rank ducked as he jumped over them into the shrinking center. Inside the square the stench of powder and burnt cartridge paper was overpowering. Piles of dead littered the ground and the field doctor labored over an officer whose blood soaked into the grass around him.

Realizing it was Kendall, Matt ran to kneel beside him.

The merry green eyes were dull with pain. "Matt, thank God you're here," Kendall gasped. Weak fingers covered with blood grasped Matt's sleeve. "My juniors all dead. Don't let my men lose heart, Matt."

"They will stand, Kendall, I promise." He squeezed his friend's hand, and with a sigh, Kendall closed his eyes.

Matt stood and glared at the doctor. "Do not let Lord Kendall die!"

The blood-and dirt-streaked face stared back at him. "His wounds are grievous, my lord."

"He will live, do you understand!" Matt commanded.

141

Finally the doctor nodded. "Yes, my lord. I will do my best."

For a heartbeat Matt was back at Fort McHenry with Jeffries dying, his body protecting Matt from the enemy; Higgens rising up with his last breath to rally the men; his men moaning in death all around him. For what purpose? He understood now, for Serena had helped him find his way. Serena. There was so much left unsaid.

Holding the thought of Serena, he rallied the men with cries of home, bolstering their courage.

As each man fell, the square tightened, leaving no place open. The front rank knelt, the butt of their muskets on the ground, bayonets in place to slash at the cavalry horses; the two ranks behind with muskets poised and loaded, ready to fire and reload alternately, had already thinned out. Matt urged the front man to reload for the man behind him.

The cavalry charged a third time, but Picton's regulars held. By nightfall Quatre Bras was declared a stalemate. Matt didn't question the grievous loss. He knew its purpose. They had delayed just long enough to take the wind out of ol' Boney's sneak attack and allow the duke to find his ground.

Kendall lived still, although his gray color beneath the bloody sandy curls sent cold dread to coil tightly around Matt's heart.

"I won't let you die, Kendall," he promised, but his friend couldn't hear him.

The doctor, however, did. "If you wish Lord Kendall to survive, we must get him to Brussels immediately."

"Keep him safe," Matt demanded. "I shall return."

Wellington had set up headquarters at Genappe between Quatre Bras and La Haye Sainte. It was there Matt presented his report and stood with Uxbridge as Wellington spread out the map.

"Picton must fall back from Quatre Bras because Blücher and the Prussians have retreated eighteen miles to Wavre. We will have to stop the French here." With a pen he circled a spot beyond Mont St. Jean called Waterloo. "Here is where we shall meet," he declared. "Blackwood, notify Picton to fall back. He won't be pleased."

"I shall leave as soon as a fresh mount can be saddled. However, I request a wagon. Kendall has fallen. I want him sent back to Brussels without delay."

Wellington shook his head, the piercing eyes studying Matt's face. "Kendall down! A good man. He'll be missed. Take what you need. Enter!" he barked to a knock at the door.

Shock rooted Matt to the spot as his brother strode into the room. "Long, what do you here!"

"Sorry, Blackwood, forgot to tell you the marquess brought dispatches from London for me. Could use your services a bit more, Longford. Seems my communication system has broken down. Need a swift, steady rider along the right flank tomorrow. Think your brother can handle it, Blackwood? Not a soldier, after all."

Matt stared at Long's impassive face. "My brother is the finest horseman in all of England." "I know." The duke laughed, slapping Longford soundly on the back. "I've won a monkey half a dozen times myself on you at White's."

"Then Your Grace must be aware the betting book at White's predicts I shall meet my end on one of my wild horses," Long drawled, flicking the duke a hooded glance.

"You must hoodwink them, Longford. For tomorrow I shall need every good man I can find. Now, Blackwood, you have your orders."

"Your Grace, since Longford won't be needed until tomorrow, he could transport Kendall back to Brussels."

"See to it," the duke barked, striding from the room.

"What has happened?" Long asked, with no trace of boredom.

"Kendall has fallen. You must get him back to Brussels and get him medical help."

"I shall take him to Serena. She stays with Cecily and Mrs. Buckle at Lady Charlesworth's. Those three could drag a man back from hell if they set their minds to it."

His heart gave one single stroke. "Serena? Here? How? Why?"

"Steady, Matt. You shall ask her yourself." The familiar

mocking smile curved Long's mouth. "But first, I believe Wellington gave you an order."

Shocked that thoughts of his wife could make him so forget himself, Matt moved with superhuman speed procuring a wagon and driver and urging Longford toward Quatre Bras. He left him with precise directions to Kendall's regiment while he continued on with orders for Picton.

The old man was not happy, as Wellington had foreseen. Holding his hand firmly to his two broken ribs, Picton cursed and raved, but in the end followed the orders as he'd always intended.

Weary soldiers tramped along the chausée. Occasionally a snatch of song could be heard. Matt searched for Kendall's brigade and found them near the front, two newly appointed officers reorganizing their march. He learned Long had left only an hour before him. He spurred his horse forward, searching the mass movement for signs of a wagon. It was slow going as the army shifted their position for the coming battle. Finally he saw Long up ahead. The wagon jarred to a stop and Matt dismounted to reassure himself Kendall still lived.

His lids slowly lifted. The haze over the usually bright eyes pierced Matt like a bullet.

"Longford here. What a lark, hey, Matt?" Kendall tried to grin, but it turned into a grimace of pain.

"Easy, old friend. Long shall take you to Brussels. To Serena and Cecily."

Slowly he rolled his head to where Long stood beside the wagon. "Long, if ... if I don't make it—" Kendall swallowed, taking a harsh breath "—Tell your sister she's stolen my heart."

"Tell her yourself, Kendall," Long snorted. "And a merry dance she'll lead you."

"I ... can hardly wait," Kendall sighed, closing his eyes, with a shadow of his old grin.

At just that minute the threatening gray clouds overhead split, and pelting rain began to fall. Matt swept his cape off his shoulders and flung it over Kendall, protecting him as best he could from the downpour. If he developed a fever...

"Long..." Fear for his friend colored his voice. He couldn't let Kendall die like Jeffries, Higgens, and the others.

"Never fear, Matt, I won't let Kendall die. God in heaven, I couldn't bear the peal Cecily would ring over me for the rest of my days."

Grasping his brother's shoulder, Matt stared into the hooded eyes. "I know not what tomorrow will bring. Tell Serena—"

"Good God, not you, too!" Long exploded, stopping Matt cold. "God continue to preserve me from cupid's arrow! You shall tell her yourself. Believe that!"

Longford leapt back onto his horse, and with a wave of his hand, the wagon creaked away, leaving Matt staring after it.

Lightning split the sky, and a second later, thunder rumbled around him. The storm was at hand. If he lived through it, he would tell Serena all that was in his heart.

Her heart jumped to her throat when word reached her in the front parlor, where she sat under Buckle's guidance rolling bandages, that the marquess had returned with an injured officer.

She raced, with Cecily at her heels, to the back courtyard.

When she saw Kendall's ashen face and blood-soaked uniform, she clasped her hand over her mouth to still the nausea. Beside her, Cecily broke into loud, gasping sobs.

As three footman lifted Kendall's limp body from the wagon, Aunt Lavinia, Frederick, and Buckle all appeared in the doorway.

"Lord Charlesworth, go fetch a doctor immediately," Buckle urged, and to Serena's surprise, Frederick instantly did as she bid.

With her owl eyes blinking rapidly, Aunt Lavinia wrung her hands. "The blue bedroom," she finally gasped, bustling away.

When Kendall, face and uniform black with soot and dried blood, was carried past them, Cecily recoiled with horror back against the house.

"Come, Cecily, we must attend him until the doctor arrives," Serena said gently, touching her arm.

"No!" She shrugged her hand away. "I can't! He looks so ...

so…" Cecily's eyes were round with horror.

Raging anger exploded through Serena's veins. Gripping Cecily's shoulders, she shook her. "This is what a hero of the nation looks like! Remember what you said! It isn't glorious and it isn't noble! He no longer looks like your glittering dream hero, does he? He looks like a man who has fought bravely for his country. Which do you truly love, Cecily, your dream of him or the man he truly is?"

Cecily shook with her sobs while tears ran unceasingly down her cheeks. "The man, Serena, the man!" she cried, tearing out of Serena's grip to race after him.

"I shall see to him until you arrive, Serena," Buckle said calmly from the door before following Cecily.

Alone with Longford, Serena turned to look at him. The dark hair was tumbled over the chiseled forehead. Mud clung to his usually impeccable clothing and caked his Hessians.

"Longford, what of Matt?" Finally she asked the question that drove her through each hour of this interminable wait.

"He is well. We parted near Genappe. He ordered me not to let Kendall die. I promised him we wouldn't."

"I shall keep your promise," she declared hoarsely, unshed tears choking her throat. "What is happening?"

"They held the French at Quatre Bras. But tomorrow will be the great confrontation." He shrugged. "And that outcome only God knows."

Climbing back on his horse, Longford stared down at her. "I must get back. Will you be all right here? There is panic in the city."

Lifting her chin, she stared back at him. "Don't concern yourself about us."

He laughed with that genuine note which was so rare. "I told Matt, between you, Cecily, and Buckle, the devil should beware."

"The next time you see Matt, tell him—"

"No!" he bit out. "You shall tell him yourself, I promise," he declared grimly, wheeling his horse and galloping away, leaving her staring after him.

Yes, she must tell him herself. If only she was given

another chance!

Fear settled firmly into the fabric of her being. Fear that she'd never have the chance to say the words which burned in her heart.

She loved him. Forever.

The Love Match

Throughout the long evening, Serena paced in the hallway outside Kendall's room. Cecily sat in a straight-backed chair against the wall, not daring to move or make a sound until the surgeon came out with a report. Occasionally into the silence fell a low moan, and Cecily's knuckles whitened. But since Serena asked the all-important question, Cecily's resolve had never faltered.

As the door finally opened, both women held their breath.

The doctor rolled down his shirt-sleeves and stared at them with red, tired eyes. "I've removed two bullets, one from the chest, and another from his arm. For a while I debated taking the arm, but his lordship assured me he'd have my head if I tried."

"I must see him!" Cecily sobbed.

"He's asleep now, miss, and probably will remain that way for some time."

Cecily could wait no longer and flew past the doctor to see Kendall for herself.

"That man has lost much blood." Beckoning Serena aside, he lowered his voice. "I don't know what will be the outcome of his lordship's wounds. Have you someone who can nurse him? There is no one I can send. The city is in chaos."

"We can do it, if you just give us directions." She was determined to keep Kendall safe. Somehow, although her mind knew it couldn't be so, she had equated saving Kendall with keeping Matt safe on the battlefield.

"Expect a fever." The doctor walked down the hall, giving her explicit instructions and a promise to return early the next morning. But tonight they must carry on alone.

Carry on. Yes, she must carry on as Matt would expect her to do. Matt, where are you! her spirit cried. Could he feel all the love and strength she was sending his way? At least he knew she was here, she had come to be with him. Did he understand what that meant? Could he ever forgive her harsh words of parting?

She could only wait and hope for the chance to tell him what was in her heart.

Buckle with her calm good sense allowed the girls to sit quietly in Kendall's room as he slept. They rolled lint bandages before the fire, scarcely daring to whisper. At dawn Cecily fell into a fretful slumber, slumped in a chair pulled next to Kendall's bed. On the other side Buckle kept her vigil, the doctor's instructions she and Serena had discussed committed to memory.

Pushing the drawn draperies aside just enough to see, Serena watched the sun rise. Matt would already be up and about on this day—a day of destiny, and only God knew the outcome.

At six sharp, Matt was on horseback. The staff had gathered around Wellington for a final briefing. Even though he issued specific orders, he liked to give his men an overall picture so they could act for him, if necessary.

He sat his charger, Copenhagen, with every sign of ease and confidence, resplendent in white buckskin, with tasseled top boots, short spurs, a white stock, blue coat over a knotted gold sash, and a Spanish field marshal blue cape. The staff had warned him too many times that he made an excellent target than to do so again.

Matt remembered from the Peninsula the duke didn't like to get wet. Even though the sky had cleared, he was taking no chances. He wore a cocked hat similar to Napoleon's, Matt thought eccentrically, although he wore it fore and aft instead of broadside. Stuck in the hat were the four colored cockades signifying Britain, Spain, Portugal, and the Netherlands.

The staff had swollen to forty, regulars and those specially requested like Longford, and hangers-on. Where was Longford, anyway? Matt wanted to know about Kendall.

The duke took up a position under a lone tree at the crossroads staring across the rain-soaked ground, now a quagmire of watery puddles and mud to the thousands of French who faced them.

Suddenly Matt heard the faint ringing of church bells off in the distance. It was Sunday. In Brussels and in all the surrounding villages, people would be attending church, praying for victory this day.

Would Serena be among them, or would she stay at Kendall's side, offering him the gift of her strength which he so sorely needed?

A light breeze played across Matt's hair, and in the oddest way he was comforted as if he felt some of her strength himself. In every battle of his life he'd fought alone, secure in his sense of honor and duty. Now he felt something different. Although there was still so much left unsaid between them, Matt carried, at last, a true image of Serena and the rest of his world which gave him an inner peace and resolve. England, its policies and governments, might not be perfect, but it was the best he knew. He remembered his Shakespeare and found himself repeating snatches throughout the day: "This royal throne of kings, this sceptered isle, this earth of majesty ... this happy breed of men ... this blessed plot, this earth, this realm, this England." It would endure long past this day of battle, and so would he.

Sometime before twelve, fever took possession of Kendall's pain-racked body. Serena held him down, keeping his shoulders from thrashing much as she had held Matt during the nightmares, while Buckle tried to force liquid through his dry, cracked lips. Cecily constantly bathed him with a cool cloth, whispering words of love and encouragement unwittingly. They fought valiantly, seeking to stem the tide of devastation through his already weakened body.

Seeing the ever-cheerful Kendall so weak, helpless under their hands, somehow made the battle more real to her. Serena wouldn't let Kendall die! Longford had promised Matt, and she was determined to do everything in her power to keep that promise. She would fight for his life as surely as Matt and all those men who had marched with such confidence from Brussels were fighting for theirs.

At eleven-thirty the French opened fire on the farmhouse at Hougoumont. Within minutes great clouds of white smoke hung over the field, lit here and there by a column of fire. The French advanced steadily, through the orchard up to the courtyard walls. Wellington peered through his telescope, watching as the doors were forced and Macdonnell's men fought hand to hand. With a great roar, reinforcements stormed the house and pushed the French back. With an imperious wave, Wellington beckoned Matt forward. Swiftly he rode with orders to Bull's howitzers to fire over the infantry to enable it to move forward and recapture the orchard.

Such a cloud of gray smoke hovered over the field now, it was difficult to see anything clearly. The pounding of the cannons rang in Matt's ears, shutting out everything else as he rode back toward Wellington. He urged the men on as he rode among them, shouting encouragement and directions. This battle was neither noble nor glorious, but necessary, he told himself over and over. Longford had once called him a leader of men; now he wasn't sure what that meant. The infantry advanced; Matt wheeled his horse in the direction of his commander.

Chills shook Kendall's slender body. He moaned continuously. Serena watched Cecily carefully, waiting for her to break down. But she remained constant. When Kendall's clutching fingers closed over her hand, she held on to him firmly, speaking soothing words of comfort. Serena built up the fire and layered covers over his shivering body. Buckle attempted to drip warm gruel down his unresponsive throat. Thoughts of the last time Serena had fought to save a life tightened the bands of fear about her heart.

When the doctor arrived, he shook his head. "He is worse. I fear for Lord Kendall's life. There is nothing more I can do."

He stepped back before the blaze in Cecily's eyes. "Lord Kendall is not going to die! If you cannot, we will make sure of that!"

The doctor left shortly thereafter, with dire reports of the wounded streaming into the city. He made a half promise he would return that evening, but Serena sensed he believed by nightfall his services would no longer be needed. Kendall would be beyond his help.

Wrapping her arms tightly around her shoulders, she shivered with deep foreboding. What she had feared was coming to pass; everything she held dear was at stake, and she was utterly powerless before it. All she could do was fight for Kendall's life with every bit of strength and courage she and Cecily and Buckle could muster.

She went to the window to look toward where the battle even now must be raging. Matt was in the thick of it, she was certain of that. Deep inside her she sensed he was still alive; surely she would know if, if … She refused to even think the words. She must be strong for Matt. He was a soldier; now she must be one, too, facing this uncertainty and fear with the same kind of courage.

All that she could do for Matt was to send her thoughts and her love to be with him through his time of danger. And pray that they would have at least one more moment together so he would know how much she loved him.

By afternoon the infantry was in defeat. D'Erlon's French infantry had swept across the Dutch-Belgian troops and forced them all the way back to the Forest of Soignes. Matt was sent, yet again, to Picton, demanding action from his lordship. He had already lost two horses and had his hat blown off, the bullet barely missing his right ear.

Picton rode to the front of his troops, waving his sword, and roared, "Charge." The line started forward at a double pace. Picton turned to the left, calling to Kempt, "Rally the Highlanders!" At that moment he fell from his horse.

Matt rushed forward, but by the time he reached his old general, Picton was dead. Behind him he heard the charge sounded. Even in the midst of confusion it never ceased to amaze him. Ten notes climbed in threes to a long, insistent tone.

Instinctively he mounted his horse and watched in amazement as the Scots Greys swept around him like a thunderbolt, crashing into the French, carrying all before them. But they did not respond to the rally. They kept going. Although they captured two eagles and fifteen guns, they were cut off and only a handful returned. Their leader, Sir William Ponsonby, was not among them, Matt mournfully reported to Wellington.

Too many had fallen for Wellington to mourn one more. His charger swept into the thick of the fighting, Matt keeping pace beside him should a message need to be sent. When leaders fell, other men took up the rally call and led. Matt had told Serena he was a soldier, but until today, he hadn't truly known what that meant.

He could hear Wellington muttering Blücher's name. If the general didn't arrive soon with the Prussians, defeat was at hand. Finally they withdrew to a small rise and Wellington pulled out his glass to survey the field.

The heavy French cannonade made the men deaf with the sound. Matt wished he could no longer hear the pitiful cries of the wounded and dying all around him. Corpsmen tried to keep the field clear, but at times the fighting was so intense, it was virtually impossible. Wellington ordered a general reverse—only one hundred paces, it would be just enough to put them out of the reach of the cannon fire. Matt was sent to pass the word, and assure an orderly withdrawal. Before it was complete, a wave of French cavalry swept toward them.

"Prepare to receive cavalry!" Wellington roared, and the infantry formed into squares. Matt galloped down the lines shouting the order, tempering his resolve into steel. One of the final squares, already set into place, was Kendall's. The new officer waved his shako and Matt responded with a fist raised high above his head.

An early evening fog settled in, pushing down the smoke so everything was seen through a peculiar gray-white swirl. Matt rode slung low over his horse toward the left flank, where Wellington had charged after seeing signs of confusion. Another rider galloped up, recklessly exposing his whole body, and reined his horse to a rearing halt.

"The Prussians are within sight," Longford gasped.

Filthy, disheveled, a rag tied around a bloody wound on his thigh, all the bored mockery stripped away, he looked wonderful to Matt.

"Long, your leg!" Matt shouted over the din.

"It's nothing." He laughed. "The duke commanded me to hoodwink the gamesters, and I shall. Did you know your ear is bleeding all down your neck?"

Gingerly touching his right ear, Matt's fingers came away bloody. "I thought it missed me. No matter! If we can hold for the next two hours, we shall have them."

"Be careful, Matt!" Long shouted back, wheeling his horse. "I'll see you in Brussels!"

Brussels, where Serena waited. In the oddest way he'd felt her beside him all this day; almost as if he were within reach of her thoughts.

If he got another chance, he would tell her what he should have said that last morning. He had fallen in love twice in his life, and both times with the same woman. The person he once was, and the person he had become, each loved her with a completeness he'd only discovered possible throughout this long day.

If he was given the chance, he would tell her. But time was running out. The Prussians were coming, but until they arrived, Wellington ordered "hold to the last man," and that they must do or perish.

By early evening, after an afternoon that left all three women drained, Kendall's fever broke. Although his breathing was still not as strong as Serena would like, tears sprang to her eyes at the doctor's satisfied nod.

"I don't know how you did it, but it seems Lord Kendall will live."

"Of course he will," Cecily stated firmly, although her soft lips quivered. "I plan to be Lord Kendall's bride."

The doctor's eyes flicked over Cecily's white-gold curls hanging in damp ringlets against her cheeks and neck, and her sherry eyes blazing in her colorless little face, and then he smiled.

"Had I known that, my dear, I would have had no doubt of his full recovery."

Hearing his kind words, Cecily slumped back down in the chair, and picking up Kendall's hand, wept all over it.

Now that Kendall was out of danger, new energy sent Serena out into the street seeking news. A surprisingly helpful Frederick was beside her. He had forsaken his ridiculous attire and airs, and with a sheepish "That all seems a bit out of place, considering," escorted her to the Brandenburg Gate.

The city was wild with conflicting reports; some claimed a French victory, then just as quickly an English. Just as the whispers had built in a crescendo around her at the Duchess of Richmond's ball only three nights before, when it seemed a lifetime ago, so the crowds shouted to each other.

"Hook-nose beat Boney once and for all!"

"It's over, let us flee at once."

"…but the cost was high."

"The French are on their way…"

Serena could not find a reliable report. She remained at the gate, long after Frederick begged her to return home. Wagons full of wounded poured into the city, their stories as conflicting as the rumors. Resigned, Serena returned home.

She sent a dozen footmen, and even the superior little butler, Andre, all over the city for news of Matt or Longford. When she could learn nothing, she became so frustrated, she actually broke down in tears for a moment, shocking Aunt Lavinia so much, she did the same.

Her aunt was put to bed by her solicitous maid and Buckle, who informed Serena she always knew Lavinia had a heart, it was just so very well hidden.

It was just as well Aunt Lavinia had succumbed to tears, for surely she would have fallen into a fit of the vapors had she witnessed Serena convincing her cousin Frederick to accompany her to the battlefield.

"Serena, it just isn't the thing," he protested, his owl eyes nearly starting from his head.

"Frederick, I can't bear another moment of this waiting!" Fear drove her to desperate measures. "If you won't go, I shall go alone, I promise you."

She could see from the horrified glaze in his eyes, he believed her. "I need an hour to get a wagon and team together. Then I'll take you," he sighed, shaking his head. "Thankfully Mother has taken to her bed."

Serena echoed those sentiments, grateful that Cecily had fallen into an exhausted slumber curled up beside Kendall's bed, his hand firmly clasped on her lap, and Buckle was also deeply asleep, so could not witness her departure in the early dawn.

During the long, torturous hours of this wait, she'd discovered what it was to be a soldier's wife. She refused to consider the reasons Matt had not returned from his duties. With courage and a sense of purpose, she set out to find him.

The roads were glutted with traffic. As each wagonful of wounded passed, Frederick would ask if it carried Lord Blackwood of Wellington's staff. Waiting for each reply, Serena folded her hands and offered a silent prayer, for what she wasn't certain. Should she pray to find Matt among the wounded or should she pray for a miracle?

She was not alone in her search for a loved one. Others searched the roadside on foot, calling out names. Equipment had been abandoned and horses roamed aimlessly, some of them limping and wounded.

They had just cleared the Forest of Soignes when she thought she saw a familiar figure. Against the rising sun she couldn't be certain. "Frederick, stop!" she commanded. She stood as he jerked the wagon to a halt. Relief surged through her, combining with fatigue to make her light-headed.

"Long!" She swayed a little as she waved. "Long! Long! It is you!"

He fought his way through the traffic to her side, his filthy face set in rigid disapproval. "My God, Serena, have you taken leave of your senses? Where do you think you're going?"

"I must find Matt! Have you seen him? Please, I must find him." Still standing in the wagon, she grabbed his bridle. "I must talk to him! You promised me I'd have the chance."

She'd never seen the dark eyes so haunted. "I've been looking myself. The battlefield is chaos. They've been shooting looters all night. This is no place for you!" He looked around her. "Who was fool enough to bring you here?" Flicking a glance at Frederick, Long gave a crack of derisive laughter. "Good God, Charlesworth, I hardly recognize you."

"Longford." He nodded. "Seemed like the right thing to do, bringing Serena. She vowed she'd come by herself." His owl eyes blinked rapidly. "I've discovered these women are quite determined females."

"Very perceptive of you, Charlesworth." With his old mocking smile, he stared into Serena's set face. "I see I can do no less than accompany you. But I warn you, Serena, you won't like what you see."

Long had never spoken truer. As they approached the battlefield, the smell of smoke mingled with the stench of blood forced Serena to place her hands over her mouth. Long turned aside more than once to put some poor miserable animal out of its misery. Tears ran unnoticed down her cheeks. There were bodies everywhere, piles of dead and pitiful wounded who cried out for mercy. Most of them had lain untended on the ground overnight.

Broken cannon, some with the barrels melted to a grotesque mass of metal, blocked their way. Here and there a horse wandered aimlessly, its rider fallen who knew where. Finally up ahead there seemed to be a semblance of order. A detail of men flung dead bodies into the back of a wagon, while another group hardly any more carefully shifted wounded men into a hospital cart.

With horror surrounding her, she finally understood all that haunted Matt's dreams. Only the absolute belief these men had been sacrificed for a just cause made it at all bearable.

She hoped it would never have to happen again. She wasn't certain she could hold on to her courage if Matt had to go through this another time. Perhaps she lacked whatever it was that drove a man to defend his country.

She screamed in shock. A man lay facedown in the ditch, his dark hair streaming out over the regimental jacket that Matt wore. Frederick barely halted the horses before she slid out of the wagon and started forward.

"Hold her, Charlesworth, while I look," Longford shouted, his eyes hard as granite.

Frederick, with arms stronger than she'd ever have believed, cradled her against him as Long kneeled beside the body. She saw him take a long, deep breath before he slowly reached out his hand and turned the dead man over.

She saw the answer in his relief before she heard his words. "It's not Matt, thank God!"

He'd only taken a few paces before they all heard a shout for help. Off in the distance they could see two men, one blinded and the other limping, struggling toward their wagon.

"Serena, stay put! Charlesworth, come with me!" Longford commanded, and both men ran to offer aid.

Serena leaned weakly against the wagon wheel and sobbed, almost numb to pain. It couldn't end like this! She would keep going, keep searching, forever until she found him.

They had only had a beginning. He didn't know she loved him. She would give her hope of heaven to have but one more moment—one more moment to tell him.

Her gaze lifted from where Long and Frederick helped the two soldiers, to blindly scan the field, looking where she could search next. On a slight rise, silhouetted black against the rising sun, one figure stood out. He gestured, obviously giving orders to other men moving around him. But it was that one commanding figure which brought Serena upright.

There was a certain breadth to his shoulders, the way the sun shot gold through his hair, that made her take a step forward, and then another, and another.

Ignoring Long's shouts behind her, she stumbled on, unmindful of all that lay beneath her feet.

Shading her eyes from the sun, she saw the figure more

clearly in profile, and then she began to run.

"Matt!" she sobbed, and then again, "Matt!" she cried through a throat choked with tears of joy.

He whirled and saw her, his eyes widening in shock and ultimately joy; eyes full of all the answers she'd ever need.

"Sweetheart!" He caught her with hands that locked them together. He slid his fingers into her hair and sought her mouth like a man dying of thirst seeks water.

She clung to him, whispering words of love onto his lips, his cheeks, his eyelids, and received them in turn.

He cupped her tear-streaked face with his hands, his thumbs caressing her trembling lower lip. His eyes, no longer unfathomable, searched hers. "I feared I'd never get this chance to tell you I love you in ways I've just begun to understand."

She turned her lips into his palm and kissed it. Cupping it against her cheek, she looked up into those eyes which so long ago had first drawn her. "We're the lucky ones. We have been given another chance."

He pulled her tightly within the haven of his arms. "It's not chance at all, sweetheart. In every battle I've ever fought, I've been alone. But today I could feel you beside me, feel your love reaching out to me."

At last a joyous peace settled into Serena's heart and she knew that of all their beginnings, this was the one of love.

Also by Sherrill Bodine

THE DUKE'S DECEIT

What if living a lie gives you the life you want to live?

Mary Masterton is a desperate woman. Facing the advances of loathsome suitor she can't imagine marrying, she is short on choices. She convinces a handsome stranger, the victim of a head injury, that they are engaged. Left with no memory of his previous life, the man has no reason to doubt her.

The man's signet ring is the only clue to his true identity as the Duke of Avalon. Determined to reclaim his past, he begs Mary to accompany him on a journey to track down the meaning of the ring. Once more Mary finds herself in a hopeless situation: help the man she has come to love and risk losing him forever, or keep him in the dark and live a blissful lie…

THE RAKE'S REDEMPTION

Love can come crashing into your life when you least expect it.

After the sudden death of his parents, Dominic, the Marquis of Aubrey, has inherited a prestigious title, abundant wealth, and a life of luxury. On his way to London to mark the start of another social season with drinking and carousing, his travels are interrupted by a collision with a young widow's carriage.

Juliana Grenville, still mourning the death of her husband, prepares to help her overworked brother find a wife when the infamous Marquis crashes into her life. Intrigued by his secretive manner and dark past, she finds herself drawn into his world, even as both try to resist the growing passion between them.

SCANDAL'S CHILD

True love is often scandalous…

As her brother and sister prepare to make their Society debut, Kat Thistlewait vows to sit on the sidelines like a proper young lady. Fate has other plans, though, and when Kat tries to save her mischievous twin she lands herself in a compromising position with battle-scarred and world-weary French nobleman Jules Devereaux.

Knowing that no lady of quality would ever overlook his imperfections, Jules agrees to marry Kat in order to save what little reputation she has left. A marriage of convenience isn't what either desires, but love can grow from the most unlikely of sources.

THE CHRISTMAS BALL

The perfect Christmas gift can be found under the mistletoe.

Outshone by a gregarious stepsister and overbearing stepmother, Lady Athena Cummins is used to fading into the shadows. Beloved only by her youngest sister Persephone, Athena has accepted her destiny as a spinster. But Persephone has a different scheme in mind, and conspires to send Athena out for one night of fun at Lord Finchley's masquerade Christmas Ball. The masked beauty catches the Lord's eye but, determined to avoid the wrath of her stepsister, Athena leads Lord Finchley on a wild chase to discover her true identity.

MY LORD'S LADY

For a Lord and a Lady, familiarity breeds contempt—and they are about to get very familiar.

Brought together at the start of the London social season, Lady Georgina and Lord Vane are immediately at odds. The Lord's cool countenance annoys Georgina to no end, while Lord Vane has no desire for his orderly routine to be upended by the passionate Lady Georgina. Forced together while under quarantine, will they overcome their mutual dislike? Are they destined to be at each other's throats…or lips?